GL

A YEAR AT RIVER MOUNTAIN

Also by Michael Kenyon

Fiction

The Beautiful Children (Thistledown Press, 2009)
The Biggest Animals (Thistledown Press, 2006)
Durable Tumblers (Oolichan Books, 1996)
Pinocchio's Wife (Oberon, 1992)
Kleinberg (Oolichan Books, 1991)

Poetry

The Last House (Brick Books, 2009)
The Sutler (Brick Books, 2005)
Rack of Lamb (Brick Books, 1991)

A YEAR AT RIVER MOUNTAIN

MICHAEL KENYON

thistledown press

Thistledown Press Ltd.
118 - 20th Street West
Saskatoon, Saskatchewan, S7M 0W6
www.thistledownpress.com

Library and Archives Canada Cataloguing in Publication

Kenyon, Michael, 1953-
A year at River Mountain / Michael Kenyon.
Issued also in electronic format.

ISBN 978-1-927068-04-5
I. Title.

PS8571.E67Y43 2012   C813'.54   C2012-904710-4

Cover and book design by Jackie Forrie
Printed and bound in Canada

Canada Council   Conseil des Arts   SASKATCHEWAN   Canadian   Patrimoine
for the Arts   du Canada   ARTS BOARD   Heritage   canadien

Thistledown Press gratefully acknowledges the financial assistance of the Canada
Council for the Arts, the Saskatchewan Arts Board, and the Government of Canada
through the Canada Book Fund for its publishing program.

Thanks to my teachers, both in the world and in the great flow. Thanks to Seán Virgo for editorial support and friendship.

For Lorraine

And here memory, that ingenious stage director, performs one of its impossible, magical scene-changes, splicing two different occasions with bland disregard for setting, props or costumes.
— *John Banville*

If there is no changing of images, no unexpected merging of images, there is no imagination and the act of imagining does not occur.
— *Gaston Bachelard*

AUGUST

Middle Palace   Yin Metal

THE VALLEY RUNS WEST AND EAST and the temple is on the small
hill on the north side, the hill being, so we think, so they say, a
stone eye that fell from the mountain, biggest of the chain that
rises behind River Mountain Monastery. The hills to the south
are many and rounded and carry on their backs a green carpet
of trees over which the sun and moon travel left to right. There
is an immense plain south of those hills, blue smoky horizon
to grey smoky horizon. The west part of our valley this side of
the river is wet, much of it marsh in winter, full of bamboo and
birds and creatures who prefer their feet wet or whose lifecycle
involves a spell in the water. Streams crisscross the northern
slopes, though most are dry at this season, the most faithful
pouring spring water past the doors of our huts and shrines into
the river as it cuts through the yellowing fields and gleams now
on its way to the gorge and the eastern coast. We farm the fertile
banks and tend the higher rice terraces. From the winding river
to the temple behind me runs an ancient path, on and up the
mountain, used by miners, then by itinerant priests and sages,

long before the founding of our order. The wind is huffing among our buildings and bright clouds sortie across the sky.

This is where we live, for the most part, in a village of huts above the plum trees, unless we are in retreat on the mountain or on a journey somewhere to enlarge our souls. And our life here is divided. Our south-facing selves attend every flicker of change, while at prayer in the temple, we face north and darkness, barely alive to events in the world or even on the river.

CLOUD GATE

You will perhaps want to know how I got here, where exactly here is; you will want to know what I'm doing. I have offered my description of the valley, the hill and the mountain; the chain behind still holds snow, even now at hottest summer. I have been in a state since last August, when I realized that a woman (the woman we are expecting within the month) had bewildered me. My peaceful life here, you see, has been disturbed by eagerness. We are never quite as clumsy as when we are at the end of another identity, another role, the final performance, wanting the run to continue, yet tired of the same old entrances and exits, wanting to press forward with a new part, yet pulling back at the same time, regretting the past. The company of the company. There we are in the theatre seats, waiting for our notes, the director midstage, hub of the wheel. What a world! Waiting for the spark to ignite us, bind us together. It is what has formed around me here, monks for players, master for director. I sense I'm not the only one bent during prayer, head cocked like a bird, listening for Imogen's approach. Last year we were bereft, even the master, when she left us to go back to her country, leaving her trace in any number of cities on the way, for she never rests long in one place.

I know I'm extremely foolish, believe me. You will be pleased to hear that. I think you will be pleased. I want to please you because you once loved me, and I always like to please those who loved me. Perhaps you remember me from a play or from a film?

Here none of us have names, which means it will be difficult for you to keep track. When I speak of someone it will be in terms of role or function, or of specific point combinations, deficiencies and excesses of energy along certain meridians. Teaching happens in silence, through copying and practice: a double hander where one tracks a pattern in the other's body and reads the feedback. The monastery grounds are a contrived echo of our human mysteries and frailties. In fact, long ago the old gods made a copy of the mountains and rivers and the first monks built a wall around it and now, off-limits to all but the gardeners and the master, this garden contains the secrets of the order, laid out in paths and bridges and sculptures and plantings. The tasks of the gardener monks are as mysterious as the garden itself.

The walled garden. The wild lands. The paths between shrines. The gates.

The monastery is a delicate mechanism and each of us must function according to his special gifts and potentials. We are at a tipping point in our destiny. There is much accumulated darkness among the peoples of the world.

Monks disturbed in their lives are left alone, and spend their time in one of the remote shrines or in the storehouse's empty room. So it is with me. I have retreated to West Shrine. When Imogen comes again, at her usual time, soon now, I will be clear again and able to complete the rounds and routines of my days and nights, and participate in the vigils, prayers, practices, chores, without being jittery and anxious.

Often I hear the sound of water slapping, as if against the thin wooden hull of an old ship; perhaps it is a heron in the walled garden; perhaps it is the memory of Active Pass or of last spring's floodwaters against the underside of the bridge deck.

A half-moon hangs in the sky and a cricket is chirring. It feels comfortable and natural to be writing, near to the oil lamp with its constellation of flying bugs, under the stars, to someone beyond this world.

Sky Mansion

Easy to hold these two points — Sky Mansion, the window of heaven below each underarm and *Guimen*, Ghost Gate, slightly forward and to either side of the top of the cranium. First one side of the body, then the other.

The bronze bell wakes us at four in the morning for prayers and silken movements and meditation, our daily study of the pathways of the elements. We eat as the sun rises, then some of us work in the fields, some at spiritual tasks, while others copy the texts. At noon we rest and eat and pray. We walk in the forest shade to digest our food and recognise our moods folded within the day's mood. Afternoons we practice what we have studied, palpating a series of points on another monk and in turn having the series run on our own skin, and reverencing, in light of what we find, all we have learned about the human body. From a single point we derive the whole. But the whole must be woken first. We are animals with hand-paths (heart, small intestine, lung, large intestine, triple warmer, circulating sex) and foot-paths (kidney, liver, spleen, stomach, bladder, gall bladder). At the end of the afternoon we gather to chant, and evenings are for individual rituals and meetings with the master. We retire at dusk, when colour is about to drain from the world. The younger monks stay up longer because they see colour longer than those of us with grey hair and failing sight.

None of us know all the paths, deep or external, even the master. We feel our way into the body a little at a time, and feel our way out the same way so as not to get lost. Half-asleep, we glimpse the forces that crest about us. Belief is that through idleness and repetition, through prayer and compassion and through counting, each of us will unravel something surprising beneath our routines. In two weeks she will be here.

I'm a child. First I forgot matches to light my lamp, then the matches were damp and useless, so I had to go back for a lit taper, then when settled again at my little portable desk in the forest shrine I couldn't find my writing paper. Now all has been assembled the moon has set. She will come in fifteen sleeps. (Children will smile and wave their caps and bandanas.)

All day long gusts of wind have shaken the tops of trees. When wind shakes the treetops they say God is on our side. Another madman has moved into the valley, this one with his family — a woman and several children, a goat and a dog, all of them foraging today along the riverbank. They come, these madmen, quite often, in search of nourishment or wisdom, both of which can be had from our order, since it is a tradition that those in need are never turned away. They come and go, usually in summer, often when the weather is about to turn stormy. This man raves loudly at night and at times during the day. He is raving now. His screams are not in a language I understand, though some words are familiar. His anguish is unmistakeable. In the quiet dark, I shudder to think my time on earth has nearly passed.

CLASPING WHITE

She has cancelled her visit with us this year. Not just postponed for a few weeks or months as has happened in the past, but cancelled. She will not be coming for another twelve months.

We will have to wait through the rest of this summer, through autumn, winter, spring and half another summer.

Cubit Marsh

This morning a clamorous yelling from behind the trees west of the bridge. Another would rush down to the river, but I am too timid these days. Another would make his dignified way past the storehouse, through the courtyard and the trees, to confront the situation, but for certain by the time he got there the fuss would be done with, the dog beaten or the wife banished or the children gagged and locked away.

I'm dreaming of an island with four bays, each facing a different direction, each with a river or stream running into it, and if you follow each river or stream inland, you arrive at four openings in the earth near which four tribes have their villages. Each tribe holds a ceremony, one in spring, one in summer, one in autumn and one in winter, to acknowledge the darkness beyond reach of the world's weather. I'm thinking about my many lives in different parts of this planet. I often played someone quick and unobservant, someone I only vaguely believed in. But I'm playing a slow beast now, slow and meek, a dust ball tracking a silver path amid shabby bits of old fluff, and each thought shies from naming names or places, although I would like to know what we were doing when we were together, other than you a witness, me an actor. Can an intention, even if faltering, still produce the glimmer of a past event? Can the ghost of your ghost, through my obsession, show the slant of present things?

Maximum Opening

The year is closing. A heat is in the ground. Crows banter. I slept a good short sleep. My brothers this morning are calm, well adapted to their life in these hills. Soon it will be autumn and the golden time of false summer when we make our thanks-giving trek to the sea. We travel by night out of the valley, a small group of us, to visit the gorge hermit, then continue east, to the place the river meets the sea. At sunrise we will wade through the reeds to a crumbling island in the estuary where a master died long ago. We stay and fast a day before returning to prepare for the first frost.

The vanguard of winter crosses the sky on the backs of geese. It's the golden time already and I will not have the sight of her, brief as it always is, to carry to the sea.

Broken Sequence

Tonight nobody would smile at me, no one would look at me. In meditation just now the master and I were in the middle of an empty plain and in the distance was a cloud of dust, and he said, "Look closely," and I saw beneath the cloud a mass of people carrying children and pushing carts, slow as the tide, until the horizon was a clean line and what remained was billowing dust that turned silver, flattened out, went pink and disappeared. *Inconsolable.*

We murmur under the stars. In the storehouse courtyard, near the warrior tree. Still sad, I register the others chanting, their cadences, the roundness of the prayer as it rolls under the night sky.

This calm collaboration. Being solitary in community. It is all I ever really wanted. When she first came, five years ago, I was tranquil, composed, focussed; now my hair is completely grey. At sixty-eight, I'm old enough to know that most of my life is finished and what remains is to forget it or set about recording its passage. But what reason is there to give voice to mistakes made and small risks taken long ago? It only carries me into the causal stream. There's nothing brave in these notes, nothing precious, only curiosity. And a wish to be seen by a woman of whom I know little except she is beautiful.

Restless Ditch

Anger palpable in the air. This is the anger of the squirrel without enough nuts. Since the madman came others have arrived, distraught and with few belongings, to cut bamboo to make shelter, and this morning children were thronging the paths, begging, and by noon were playing in the river. When I went down to note the water level I was met by several boys and girls — I counted fourteen, though they were so quick and milling that I kept losing track — who leapt in front of me waving their hands and grinning and shouting, their clothes dirty, their faces pale and tired. Some of the smaller ones, thin with distended bellies, were crying. Afternoon is quiet yet the air still jangles. If I shut my eyes I still see their moon-faces like dabs of colour on a canvas. I'd be afraid for them, because there isn't enough food for more than ourselves for the coming winter, except I have seen these villages before, established and torn down within a few weeks, threatened by armies or gangs, and I trust the families will soon leave. Symbols of famine and catastrophe, they linger only a short time in one place, just long enough to learn of a refugee camp well supplied by an aid agency — a day's walk to the west, say, at the junction of two populous valleys, where planes can land and infrastructure still exists from earlier marches, earlier camps.

Supreme Abyss

Some things are incontestable: water droplets on the half-green leaves that fell in the night and this morning streaked the path when I swept between my shrine and the temple. I swept the dirt path clear of leaves, yet others fell around me. I stopped to listen to the birds. Last night's moon hunted a way through the clouds, clouds sent by ocean and wind, and wind hissed, still hisses, in the cedars and in the tall grass and in the bamboo.

Fish Border

Clouds fill my body sometimes. I slept well and the result is a peaceful feeling inside my body that matches the outside. The breeze cools my skin yet another breeze warms the inside of my lungs. The world is yellow, pale green, silver where sun glances off a leaf, white and grey, pale and deep blue. Inside is black, purple. A corkscrew turns through my body, down into the ground. Someone pours fluid into the top of my head. I have begun making bird nests using the abundant yellow grass, turning it, winding it, shaping each stem and weaving in pliant shoots and feathers, finishing the floor with down and moss.

Lesser Shang

I've placed the nests in trees and bushes along the paths I know she'll take (though not for twelve months), wedging each into a place least likely to be troubled by wind. I'm experimenting with different designs and materials. Some nests are no larger than a man's thumbnail and some are as big as a hipbone. I want oval pebbles to put in the nests. River stones are plentiful, but I am particular as to colour. This weaving of nests and hunting of stones involves much industry and not a little climbing and wading so these are busy days, what with prayers and sessions and meditations and this writing. Full moon now, and no sleep. We are the reeds and grasses, the lichens and mosses and river stones. The deep pattern takes in my father and mother, my race, and the West Lancashire hillside where I was born.

> *The nest is open and round so it won't*
> *hurt the fledglings or exclude dark bass or*
> *treble silver, such elements free to*
> *rise and fall together as home and cure.*
> *The nest is closed by the living presence.*
> *Time will take it from the tree. My own had*
> *a ceiling of warm feathers and a floor*
> *of twigs, dirt and once-in-a-lifetime air.*

Shang Yang

Yang Metal

PRESS YOUR THUMBNAIL INTO THE SOFT FLESH AT the corner of the nail of your first finger. Reach your other hand behind and find Ambitious Room, Bladder-52, second lumbar vertebrae, just outside the spine.

I am here because I fled what constrained me in my past life and worked the change so carefully that I don't quite know how it happened. Imogen was born in the same county as I was born and became an adult on the same continent that I became an adult. She is an actor and I was an actor. She is drawn to this place by the same forces that drew me, yet she inhabits a world I see only in memory. Sometimes I imagine she is living the life I might have lived had I not systematically misplaced every grindstone, since she still lives among money, career, family, car, travel, and houses, while I've retreated to the underbeat. Faker. Loser. I throw a bridge out to her, but the bridge has a fatal strain or fault, and the returning traffic is a puzzle. Last year she looked at me as I chanted and afterward asked me to show her the spring behind the temple. And, as early sun stabbed through the trees and lit the top leaves, we stood by the quiet pool; moisture beaded on the small fair hairs on her arms.

Ah. The temple bell lunges as the world tips, timber about to strike the green that clothes the bronze.

Second Space

Prayers sounded mad tonight, a wind blowing them close, then away, voices blended in the rolling dark till I was muddled up in the heat, my back against the tree, open to the long vowels especially. This is who I am now, at home in air spiced with what day left behind, and in the spice a token of what's next: cleaning the toilets. Tomorrow we move our shit to a new location, farther from the river. Last year an embankment collapsed and we lost a year of compost. A deal of digging is to be done, the old terraces leaking and the margins plugged with bamboo. There's a fear of losing the old graves since the river is changing course again. Soon it will be time for winter meetings, time to discuss the movement of water, water itself, the *qi* of water, water's presence on a moonless night, water at dawn and at noon, spit and blood, and dust on a glass, when water has evaporated, the smallest drop on an eyelash, a bubble on a dead lip — water as the river: the west mountains where it begins and the estuary to the east where it loses its silt to the sea.

> *a stone in a nest*
> *jar of water, jar of ink*
> *the river's course*

This chanting is not about who I have lost, who I have been, though it contains my wife and our boy and my small life. I was afraid to speak to others unless I was drunk or working, and when I spoke to others, drunk, working, I saw myself gazing like a child at adults; I got so dizzy I had to climb down the rickety steps, the scene over, players and audience all gone home.

THIRD SPACE

Night. How many times the gate squeals. How many shooting stars. When the crickets resume, I'm in possession of only what I feel and see. Here I know what takes place: by the season of the year, by the hour of the day. Invisible geese are flying south. The flock first, then the ideas, too many to count, though counting is important.

Farmers put away their tools, clean and oil and safely store their ploughs and scythes, what-have-you, take up the weapons cleaned and oiled and stored after the last campaign, say goodbye to their families and head south into the great plain where armies are massing.

Five hundred steps from the warrior tree to the well. If not always then more often than not. Twelve nests in the east plum trees. Thirty-two heartbeats from when a bell is struck to when its note passes into silence. I have spent the last three nights watching the river, counting leaves, trees, bamboo shoots. Counting seed heads, stars, rice grains. Counting waves from a stone.

Joining Valley

A common sight, leaves, and the sound of them underfoot every step, which is why the path must be swept twice a day, so when we go to pray we will not make a noise, unless it's the noise of our breath, or our counting in quiet voices each step, which some of us do, while others count inwardly, as I do — steps, breaths. We walk together in single file up to the temple and down again at dusk and dawn. I know the sound of each person's footfall. Today I walked behind an old monk and ahead of one of the youngest. The old man left in his wake a lingering and horrible stink. The youngster hissing something rhythmic under his breath. At first I thought the smell was my own because I had been transporting shit, but the stench increased once we were sitting inside the temple and others around the old man kept swivelling and sniffing. He is very old. His smell was disturbing because, while it included a whiff of rot, it also had in it fresh milk, or cream. I don't know what will evolve from setting this down. This smell of fruit past ripe, dying grass and latrines.

Yang Gully

The nests must be better made and more carefully secured. Several have fallen already. Some I can't find. I hoped I'd learn what home was for other animals.

Veering Passage

"Do you have any stories to tell me?" the master asked.

"A poem," I tell him.

"Written at West Shrine?"

"Yes."

"I thought stories would come."

"Not much, no."

"Too bad. I'm not in the mood for poetry."

I left him and walked down to the river. Dragonflies were splashes of blue in the rushes on the bank. Swallows were hunting, mixing up the layers of air.

Warm Flow

Now she was to be here, arrived. This morning. Dropped off by car or bus and met on the other side of the bridge and escorted over, as on other years, by the chosen monks, to the master's hut.

What about this story? A horrible scream, then barking. When we ran to investigate we found a small group assembled in a meander of the shallow river, the family that first claimed the spot now joined by others, mostly men but also a dozen women and three times that many children. A goat was dead, and a dog stood over her bloody guts. The wild dog came with the wild people. Babies were crying. The men crouched in the water, gesticulating and pointing. The children threw stones at the dog, who slowly backed away, panting in the heat.

The men sang into the night and from the fierceness of the songs, familiar from previous years, we surmised they would soon be leaving to join others on the grasslands under the banner of the local warlord. And so into battle with government forces. A number of variables will determine the campaign's outcome:

the success of this year's crop, the weight of the year's debts, the condition of the land and the quality of intelligence gathered concerning the resources of other warlords. Boundary disputes have intensified over the past few years. The dead goat is a sign of change. Another death immediately followed; a boy and a girl were found floating face-down in the river.

LOWER RIDGE

A monk found the girl and dragged her to the riverbank and revived her with heart and kidney points. He cleared her lungs, and when she coughed, he sat her up. A vulture was perched on the boy's opened body swinging gently in the reeds. The bird gazed at the monk, then re-immersed its head.

UPPER RIDGE

Mist, this evening, and then the moon rolled through. Confusion, because of the dead boy. If the world is still does chaos rise as a kind of sensitivity? Are long events coming to a head or is this the middle of a circumstance? They say death happens, but I am caught at a stone fence between two fields and can't find the stile, and it's not that I can't climb the fence, that would be easy, but the path I followed has always led to the stile and there is no stile. From here downhill and from here uphill there is no stile. Of course there is no stile. Stiles belong to England: a long stone set into the dry-stone wall at the time of its construction, easy passage through the fields, worn from years of use. I'm no longer stepping over England's stiles and ditches.

The stile would be there whether I was coming or going, over the farmer's field, to and from school. A little boy in grey shorts clambering over the stile, crossing the furrowed field, then pulling the secret plank from the brambles to set over the ditch and —

I wanted to see where the monk pulled the boy and girl from the water. Are paths the convolutions of some other energy? Some fabric I haven't got the gist of yet? The gist is what carries us, perhaps, and the stile and the plank are too real. I've shied from ideas all my life because thinking seemed too short — insufficient leverage for the truly profound — and the clever abstractions arose anyway. They rose and burst like bubbles.

A sleek crow, its violent cry. Crow in mist seeking a night perch will distract a monk, and send him, disturbed, to his room and sleep with no touchstones but these. Exile. Ex-wife. Ex-son.

The monk who brought the girl to life is euphoric.

ARM THREE MILES

Leaving the theatre was difficult. In film there was nothing to glue the days to the nights. Always drunk, I stared into the Fraser River from an embankment high above the flood plain while travelling the Sky Train. I stared up into Indian Arm while crossing Second Narrows, the Iron Workers Memorial Bridge, to and from the North Shore soundstage with my friend Jake. And that last run in Victoria — my fresh start — was horrible. I stared at the ferry's wake through Active Pass on my way back to Vancouver and felt the tug of water, cold and fast, night and day different again, but closer and closer together, black and white beads on a string.

Start counting now and it's the end of life you count toward, since work hides that. Being in the black hides death. Red gives you glimpses. Beyond debt, you're in the element of death itself. Death of your mother, then father, of everyone you know. An iron bridge, a sky train, a ferry, will give you glimpses, beyond relevance, of suicides and other leapers.

Pool at the Crook

We misunderstand the universe because the universe is all things, susceptibility to our understanding only one of them. We approach, hauling geegaws and singing, madness in disguise, and comprehension of metaphysics arrives from the rear on the backs of our children, themselves riding the shoulders of their grandparents, our own dads and mums, as they outflank us and are soon specks in the remote future. It is reasonable that I am on a hillside, near the ruined terraces of an old mining village that has long been a temple and the home of a sect of monks dedicated to the mapping of stars within the human body. It is reasonable that my life began in another country far from here and will end in yet another country. Reasonable that my constitutional condition is a high form of energy (high in the body, that is) known in the West as worry or nerves or anxiety and in the East as proximity to heaven. I do not know myself because I am all things, susceptibility to self-knowledge only one of them.

Tautology. But if I look up from the slow river past midnight and catch sight of the mountain I know something is in the wings. I am at River Mountain because I have turned my back on my family, history, country. The recent maps will not inform or marry into these old systems. They cannot. Here the personal is almost beside the point. Each star in the body is a vital indirection. Some gates open on well-oiled hinges, some loosen with a squeal. The plank and stile are missing; the well-worked field is to be contemplated, its sky to be entered backwards, to be stood under, not understood. The practitioner becomes the gate from *Where are you going?* to *Where have you gone?*

I must wait. That's all. *Wait a moment! Wait for me!* For the annual arrival of this blonde freckled woman, her shoulders holding heaven. Anxiety as excitement. As follows eternity. I have no wish to see her naked, I do wish to see her naked. It isn't possible to pose a contradiction, one thing and its opposite. Both belong to this world; they are on this side of the bridge.

My heart bobbles at the sound of a footstep on the path — a leaf has fallen since I swept — someone is approaching. It's time to circle the temple.

Before, when I lived in a house and was a member of the neighbourhood, my feet had no roots and my head was closed; there were only "tidings of comfort and joy" in the depths of winter. I thought it was dark and silent but it wasn't. I thought it was quiet and lit only by the light of stars but it wasn't. I thought I was in a wide arena of rustlings and curtain calls and co-star shadows but I wasn't. Now I live for Imogen to open the south gate and close it behind her, to bring a dimension of what I have left — all those plays and movies — and a trace of what I have lost.

ELBOW CREVICE

I left behind what I could no longer stomach. Quite literally: my stomach would not hold the food I put into my mouth. I was ready to get in line for my pension the way I'd got in line for my education, house and car, same way I'd framed a child and trusted his care to those trained in the care of children. My belly suppurated. Colitis. My liver nurtured dark rage.

Every night I and the rest of the cast and crew crossed the tracks from the dangerous end of town where immigrant clowns swallowed swords to the suburban soundstage door. I could fill this forest with the differences between theatre and camera. On the Vancouver skyline towers glittered, more each year. Every summer we rented a cottage on a bay where my wife and I and our boy would enter the sea and swim out of our depths and lie on our backs and feel the sky arching over our bellies, then return to the hot sand with its crescent of grass and planted trees, fish and chip stand. The death of this idyllic sequence sank us, but also provided release from well-paid, irrelevant movie work, my wife's failed novels, our shared comfortable poverty, debt (we borrowed heavily from the state's storehouse), and introduced the first vicious spines of a spatchcock world.

I've been here twelve years and can now find my way around the human body by touch alone.

I do not know what this place really is. I have felt a great chain of watchers behind me as I work: each sits crosslegged and the line snakes back along a wild landscape like the bones of a tail. Each watcher sits self-engrossed, yet curious about this engagement with the body my fingers sink into.

ARM FIVE MILES

The latrine system of buckets and sawdust, compost piles and straw, is elegant. Human waste is used, eventually, to fertilise the soil in which we grow our food. It is a question of practice — as in the practice of prayer — routines, cycles and time. The shit in the compost must cook, steam rising, for twenty-four hours.

UPPER ARM

We dwell in earth's heat. There is container and energy and ground. Our container, which is the body, is the yin side of energy, and starlight is the yang, and black hole the yin of starlight. Our ground is the ocean, unnameable psyche, while our death is yin. Death is yin to love's yang. Every morning we get out of bed and slip on our clothes, yin cloth for surrender, yang for defence. Up there is ground. Down there is ground.

I was on a hillside hearing the motor of this earth. Sunshine warmed my left side, especially my forehead, since my head was down. A group of monks were working farther up the hill. A voice below sang, "The sun is up and shining this morning, now red, now yellow." Slow wasps turned in eddies around my sweating ankles. "Tonight may be our last. Tonight we may close the book of life."

There is judgement in families — free floating between attachments to particular members — and it is contagious.

I love some of these men, mistrust others, but quietly. We form a miraculous whole.

The village girls are robust, small and beautiful. Imogen is another thing, blonde and waif-like. Even absent, she is a kind of guide, pointing out this and that, this icon, that text. Of course she doesn't do this literally, it's just how I think of her. She focuses something; she's not a focal point — though that of course — but a focuser, and involuntary. She's an earlier version of me, perhaps: the beginner, the neophyte, and innocent.

I wonder what remains for me to accomplish. Something new? Let me feel the answer before I make a move. I need a sign before making a declaration.

Once I was on a ferry, in the forward lounge, one hand bust, fingers of the other at rest on my laptop, watching gulls and the setting sun. A small family sat across the aisle, a mother and baby and a father and infant, the child a boy. The boy began to scream and hit his father, saying "No!" over and over. The father held him at arm's length while he screamed. The mother kept the sleeping baby. They were like two families separated by an immense distance. But I'm not free to read such images, even in this forest clearing.

SHOULDER BONE

Sometimes at the end of day nothing is to be found, neither pen nor paper, the name of the month nor the season. Not a face of anyone loved. Every surface is sticky with the end of summer, water having retreated deep behind the bark. Why would I lose my son? I gave up belonging, that's all. These hills are the cast-off hard-baked skeletons of what stood here long before miners or monks came to the valley. Deep in the earth of the human bone are eyes looking out, all too obvious in these monks. Doctors call it the immune system. Last year Imogen came plugged into an iPod.

GREAT BONE

We are all bored. I, at least, can admit boredom. The question is, is tomorrow worth waiting for? We turn a page, time listens. *Who are you now? How changed?* These are what sailors called doldrums, the pause between heartbeats, this storm and the next; kick back and relax. I slept in doorways, then made my way here. Almost, but not true. The quiet of no wind, not even a breeze to stir the bamboo.

On the mirror of my dressing room was an old photograph of doctors crossing a lawn, their feet making tracks in the dew.

I am offstage. What I do has meaning for others still in the play, whatever that is these days; accidents will be effective in turning some tide or other. I am backstage, in the green room; I won't be forgotten; still to come is some small act, perhaps a curtain call. I have a memory of learning to bow, taught by my mother and father, a long time ago. Surely it was for some purpose of their own that they stood me before them and clapped hands and whistled while I turned left and right and dipped my head. Why did I deny my child? I bare my head now, but this doesn't answer the question. Each time I bow I am bowed to. Each time I am bowed to I bow, while offstage music plays.

Whatever they are, gypsies or refugees, they danced this afternoon, down by the river while grass-fires smoked in hot light. The scene glowed red. Ah. That question. Mummy and Daddy, why did I give up on my boy? That question's old in the room of what's to come; that room will never be complete. The shadows of this room have occupied me recently. They run like rivers. The master's face. The girl who nearly drowned.

HEAVEN'S TRIPOD

The bridge is of corrugated metal over a bamboo frame; slung across the widest part of the river, it rides nine pylons in a series of swoops that give the effect of humpback hills. The cement footings are uneven, sunk into dry mud. From the middle of the bridge you can't see either end because of dust. The riverbanks are obscured by hanging dust this time of year. You can tell when someone else is on the bridge by the swaying.

I stopped still and listened. Someone else had also stopped to listen.

I was an actor. I earned my bread by acting, on the stage and before the camera.

I made a cage of my forearms and enclosed my head and rested my elbows on the railing. A shrill cry: hawk quartering the blank paddies.

On stage or on the set, I wore amulets and disguises. I required protection from nerves, inherited from my ambitious mother, who was also afraid, also an actor.

Perhaps this is a sanatorium not a monastery, this role not what I thought it was, and I am approaching the time when questions must be asked of the medical staff. There must have been interviews and assessments and family visits. In any case my pockets were full of river-stones and I started to arrange them along the corrugations of the bridge.

Support the Prominence

At the bottom of the valley the numbers are increasing, with more tents every day and at night loud and frantic music. The makeshift village sprawls on both sides of the river, scribed by tiny moving lights. Perhaps I've accomplished all I have to accomplish here. There seems nothing more to do except continue my routines and wait. It is the time of year, no doubt. The sadness of late summer.

Mouth Grain Crevice

Everything dying, only the great bell through the day to speak this valley and its forested hills. I can just hear the wind through the temple grounds shaking the small bells. The berries, past ripe, rot on green canes. My shrine is beautiful, remote, a long way west of the cultivated fields, below the masters' cave. There's a story about this clearing. A massacre took place once upon a time, men killed and women tied to trees and raped. The oldest hardwoods in the region grow around me, their trunks charred black. West Shrine is a place most of us avoid after dark. It hasn't rained for more than a month and dry leaves lie thick on the ground. The top branches stir the sky in a lazy way. At the far edge of the clearing are the bones of a deer that came to die. This morning I sat here and closed my eyes and saw a great hall, almost without limit, whose vaulted ceiling was black curved branches and whose floor was red leaves. Now geese, more geese, cross the river; their cries will turn me from the shrine and trudge me back home.

WELCOME FRAGRANCE

They are building down there in the river trees. They've been working for the past three days, hammering, sawing. A small stage, pale in the evening light, a pale rectangle in the green trees. The women have been stitching together bits and pieces for a carpet. I will walk down and talk to them.

September

Container of Tears   Yang Earth

On either side of the path to the cliff is a margin of black
bamboo around thick green tangled forest. The wild lands
quivered, green blades twirled. Quick stink of rot — dead
fawn — the dirt blazing red as I advanced, glimmering black-
red, rising with each step. I was almost there, turning back
through the memory of days with my family, filling my lungs
with spicy dust and vapour infused with that intense green.

The cliff is not obvious until the path and the forest end,
and then there's only pale wet air ahead and the river far below
rushing for the dark gorge.

Upstream there was banging and sawing; but I was too taken
with a blinding headache to consider what was going on, except
there were women working as well as men, women like giant
flowers come loose from the forest. Children swam in the river.
Their voices were with me even there, where the cliff crumbled
slightly at the edge.

Four Whites

A bellyache and no appetite. I shat everything out and got dizzy and went down to the encampment and wandered like a ghost among the villagers. They are small people with dark skins, quick to smile, not alarmed by the presence of a Westerner in monk's garb, yet not inclined to speak either. A faint rotten smell off the river. The rescued girl saw me and ran to hide. By noon I had to lie down and sleep in the shade of a big river tree. *What?* I woke up asking myself. *What is it?*

I vomited all afternoon.

Great Crevice

Slept under the stars with three other monks. Woke in terror to footsteps in the fallen leaves. It must have been midnight. I lay bathed in sweat, trembling and prepared for assassins, and saw soft animal faces among the branches and the stars and remembered the fawn on the cliff path two days ago, her eyes black with flies. She had not been dead long; she had not lived long either, perhaps four months. A kind of circular song shook my body until morning.

I had a conversation with a young woman on the bridge. She and I were crossing in opposite directions. For my part, I was coming back from collecting supplies from the bus; she was leaving the settlement for some guilty occupation, or so it seemed from the way she hurried, and kept her eyes on the corrugated deck, only looking up at the last moment.

She stopped and said, "You are ill." In her small dark face was the ripple of a question. Perhaps just concern. Perhaps fear: she was in the territory of men who do not farm or go out to hunt.

"Yes. I am feeling unwell."

"I hope you will soon feel better," she said.

We stood still. I set down my load. A warm fragrant breeze blew from the fields. Dust swept against our faces. We turned together to listen to it hiss through the river trees.

"Do you hear a child singing?" she said.

"It's only wind in the cables."

We stepped to the edge, our clothes flapping.

"It is in the river," she said. "Up there." She pointed upstream at a distant tangle of branches and bamboo. "Where my son drowned." She looked at me in fierce sorrow and turned away. I watched her cross the bridge to the road and disappear.

What sights we witnessed in each other on that bridge under the weight of a child's death. And she was beautiful, proud, hurt, angry. Beneath me the current had wrapped a blue plastic bag around one of the pylons.

Earth Granary

The settlement woman was probably twenty-six or twenty-seven though she carried her small dense slender body with the self-conscious ferocity of a girl. Her face and arms, especially her neck, were dusky, such a contrast to Imogen's fair skin. Just now a heron laughed. I am not myself. I'm cold, then hot. My stomach and sides and upper arms have a bright red rash, though the nausea has passed. I'm concerned to know whether she has returned to this side of the river, my imagination fired by images of her meeting a lover or an enemy alone on the desolate country road. Delirium draws me to embroider the story with darker shades of violence. Actors play out such stories in discrete, disjoint, feverish units, making films.

A moment ago the bell sounded the start of night. Down below, a circle of torches burns, voices and drumbeats rising into the air, fading and surging with the intermittent wind.

Now it is quiet but for the occasional laughter and yowls and hoots of men.

In my hot fevered state I sense invasion, forced change, instability. Six crushed beer cans found under the old cedar above East Shrine have fed my new fear of roving gangs. Some of these men are not as poor as they seem and are venturing freely through our community and onto the lower slopes of the mountain. Unfamiliar, unwelcome, especially when we're preparing for autumn.

The master told me I was about to do something sacred or forbidden, but he would not say what. Something to dispel wind-heat. Sitting with him earlier this evening, I was light-headed.

"Do you know what you will do?" he said.

"I feel like buying cigarettes."

He laughed.

"Or perhaps I need to get rid of something."

The master said to calm my thoughts and loosen my robe. "I will balance your body." He lit a candle and I undid my clothes. The rash on my chest was a range of angry red hills on a white plain. What strange diminishing fevers! Then I felt complete, seamless, as though death might be tomorrow, death the next turn, the new direction.

GREAT WELCOME

A slim woman in a short black dress and her arms full, slung her hip against the edge of her car door to slam it shut, the action turning her toward me; her complicit grin was outside time, outside language. Now it's tucked safe in memory's closet to be brought out on an occasion like this. The end of summer. The first day of school. I was on my bike and just aware of women's bodies and hers was young and wise and poised and wide open: hip shot for balance, leg extended, knee bent; inches of thigh.

What else?

A woman in a black dress. A glossy black car. A flurry of forbidden activity. A leap of some kind, then, over something my father had already tamed.

Jaw Bone

There you are. My goodness. Audience member, reader, witness. I'm cool again and safe for now from external pernicious influences, and remembering my wife's cunt, how it opened when I sat before it, that beautiful cowled monk above the petal gate — surely the point of points when all the channels are singing! I won't see another, not in that glorious way.

Curlicues of river current are repeated in the heated air. My chills were simple echoes of what is always spinning through the breezes and mirages. My body knew women's bodies. My body used to know my mother's body. And my wife's body was the strategic bridge from that past to this future.

Women are agents or spies; they travel without portfolios. What a mood I'm in! And what about children? These children are a reminder of my own child. They are also reminders of a boy who has drowned.

Below the Joint

The water rose over the child's head and his hands shaped something delicate below the surface, some earthen artefact old as bones, a hello to darkness.

Two pretty children played by the river where cold water ran swiftly at that deep place regardless the season.

Excessive cold along my spine, along the midline from sternum to pubic bone, makes me unsure I will be alive by the time Imogen comes, a year from now. This central channel reminds the body it was once a single cell dividing into two. I can feel a daily shift in my surface pulses, below which is madcap frenzy, and there are many indications of change in the valley, too, that suggest fire overacting on water. By next summer all will have changed.

The village woman's name is Song Wei. Her child, I have learned, was a boy named Suiji. He drowned after falling from a rocky outcrop when playing with his friend. Water will not wet his skin again; air will not dry him. And the girl has not spoken since the accident.

Fearful as a rabbit, I sit on my haunches and grasp the pen and write words to wake the god who will want them. The master says it is good to write. Sun on the horizon trees, the river whitely brimming. A small bell tinkles close by — one of the children. Then voices, men speaking in low tones. My brothers are at their various occupations, just as I am at mine. All of us elements in the moment beyond moments. The bell is circling me. An invisible child playing a game. *Like me, you will sicken. Like me you will heal.* My wife sickened and died, though we were already divorced. And I'm getting well again. Are you still there? Yes? Like mine does now, as I stand up to see the child, your shadow crosses the paths of others who don't notice. You cross the paths of others who love you. Like mine, your body will give up the ghost. One thing more: ghosts here are different than ghosts in the West.

HEAD'S BINDING

Today I went down to the bridge and crossed without knowing what I was doing. Crossing the bridge was like encountering resistance in a point, say triple warmer fifteen, Heavenly Crease, though the discordance was fleeting. What I have learned here is that nothing is entirely my own. Between heaven and earth, as Shakespeare knew, runs a current that we vertical ones must transmit or suffer the consequences. Put more than two of us together and we collect what the universe throws at us, but don't know what to do with it. Only two and the container has a kind of perfection. What I feel might be what you are feeling; only lifetimes of whimsy and intuition — not interpretation — will shade the difference between us. What delight and misery!

I looked down from the middle of the bridge. While not quite leaping up and waving bandanas at me, the river people, some of them children, were looking in my direction, some with expectation in their eyes. Already I recognised many, though some seemed distant, seemed to belong to other times and places.

Across the bridge, outside the monastery, I was entirely alone. Ah. If I remove myself from results then everything I do will set in motion energy along the path that needs the juice; every intersection will light up like a transit schedule.

MAN'S WELCOME

On the bridge home at noon I met someone again, not the woman but a small man, a dwarf with a large head of black hair and the blackest eyes, who was leaning over the rail scanning the water below. He'd seen me and as I approached gave me such a look that I stopped in my tracks. I waited beside him for further acknowledgement while he returned to his searching. The sun came out of the grey sky, hot on my back. The weather was unsettled. Rain had fallen in the night and it had been cloudy all day. We watched mist flowing around both banks and in and out of the forest. Perhaps he was waiting for the river to reflect these changes. We stood an hour in silence, during which time I had the feeling we were in conversation already, and it was not going well. The perfection between two beings seemed unlikely. My stomach went from unease to embarrassment, then to such shame that I couldn't move. Eventually he spoke. The sun burned deeper into my back. Hot nails into metal and fire points: pericardium, lungs, heart. I glanced down at the water and saw something float by and at the same instant the man's shoulders hunched and he got down on his knees and gripped the sharp metal edge of the bridge.

"My sister, Song Wei, has lost her husband and now her child," the dwarf whispered.

WATER PROMINENCE

We spread carpets under the plum trees in the margins of the storehouse courtyard in order to practice point location and the subtle pulses. The monk I worked on was the youngest among us. He giggled when I felt for Kunlun Mountains behind his ankle where water meets fire in the heavenly star point.

I found it difficult to concentrate. I couldn't stop thinking of the meetings on the bridge.

The boy monk had dusky skin like Song Wei's. His body had weak pulses on the left, and gall bladder felt like a kite in gusts of wind. Around us, monks were murmuring the names of points, and for a moment I got lost and couldn't feel the pattern of his deeper paths. Song Wei's face wouldn't go away. Nor would her son *Suiji*'s identical drowned face.

When it was my turn to lie on the carpet, the young monk said my pulses were big, bigger than usual, too big, like proud judges! Circulating sex, kidney, wham, wham, wham!

QI ABODE

Every morning the sun lights the bamboo outside the storehouse window; this is the first thing we see when we sit down to eat, after the body's electricity has left the core for the skin and the orifices are wide and dreams have ebbed to leave bits of image and sensation in pathways of the strange flows.

Yang bridge, couple point, Back Ravine, Small Intestine-3, edge of each hand between the root of the little finger and the wrist. I hold this, talking to heart's minister near the inner frontier gate. *How's it going?*

I kiss the jumping skin of my inside wrist and the minister responds. "Hold *qi* abode, those notches either side of Celestial Chimney, that pocket above the centre of the sternum."

The dwarf came today to ask, on behalf of the rest of the village, if they might attend the next shrine festival. I was late for meditation, on my way to the temple. He touched my hand and backed into the forest and said he wished to present a petition to the master from their counsel of elders, all of whom, he said, were women. He glanced up at me and asked for my name and I shook my head. I had another encounter with his black glistening eyes and experienced his body this time as a proud nerve encysted in dense muscle. As I looked, the muscle relaxed and black waves rolled out — physical violence, or something more dreadful.

"I am Zhou Yiyuan," he said, and bowed. "Because you have come from far away, from another country, my people think you are the one to represent our interests in the valley to your master."

"Who are your people?"

"The first to live in these valleys." He stooped and looked around, a dumb show of caution. "No one remembers that we were forced north. And now the north that nursed us has buckled and blood runs under the mountains and we are the flow manifest." And he cackled to himself: "There is no war in this country. There is no discontent in this region."

"You would like an introduction to the master?"

"Yes. At a ceremony."

"For what purpose?"

"We count on the blessings of people who understand the true position of human beings. We were farmers. Now our villages are floating. We are a remnant that acknowledges other remnants. I tell you this because you know nothing. We have been pushed farther and farther north into remote regions. Now the ground will not respond. We dwindle with each generation. It is time for us to come home."

EMPTY BASIN

"Zhou Yiyuan requests a place at the autumn festival."

The master looked at me sharply. "For himself?"

"For his people."

"All of them?"

"The elders, I think. Women."

"No." The master's willingness to hear me was at an end. "How did you meet this man?"

"His sister, Song Wei, is the mother of the drowned boy, Suiji."

The master stared at me then waved his hand. "Let another monk bring me information. These people have no names. We will not speak again." He shivered as if cold and closed his eyes. "He must be your master now. Meet with him. Meet as often as you like."

The rest of our meeting was silent. My *qi* looked out at the arrangement he had set in front of me. I could not put aside Song Wei's name or her face or her grief. And now her brother: how could this squat man's anger have anything to do with me? I felt fear ripple the surface of my skin.

QI DOOR

I remember a boy with an AK47 running down a busy street and pedestrians scattering as the boy fired at shop windows and into the crowd and at stopped cars, drivers and passengers spilling into the street. The boy began turning in a slow circle, firing bursts at those standing till most everyone was lying down, trying to crawl away or get behind a car. My wife was crying. We were both crying. We had been drinking coffee at a café, talking about the final division of property, years after our separation. This was before Amsterdam. Our own boy, who had delayed university for a job in the North Sea, was this boy's age. For days the sudden onset of tears. No control as the weeks went by. Our son's voice on the phone, at least with me, was terse and noncommittal.

Today was overcast, with cool wind whipping through the long grass in the fields by the river, hissing in the bamboo, then the lonely dry sound of crickets. On the path to West Shrine, inexplicably, I found a crumpled black robe, old and musty, with

face-like markings on one side, so I hung it in a tree beneath one
of my manufactured nests.

STOREHOUSE

"What did your master say?" Zhou Yiyuan asked.

"He won't meet you."

He leaned to one side. "People are in ignorance of what is
about to happen."

I was visiting him in his lair, a kind of lean-to at the centre
of the ramshackle settlement, and the sky drew our attention,
clouds streaming continuously westward, their patterns repeated
on the lower slopes of the mountain.

"Armies took days like this as a sign to march," he said.

"The weather is restless," I said. "How is your sister?"

"Song Wei has been sent to live alone in the forest," he said.
"Until the festival."

The villagers around us had stopped what they were doing;
they wouldn't take their eyes off me. Sunlit clouds were massing
on the southern horizon.

"The master will not allow you to attend," I told him.

"Every shift in life is accomplished by loss," he said, his eyes
cast down. "We find no footing. And yet we meet. Song Wei will
wait for you at a place of your choosing."

ROOM SCREEN

It felt as if I was swallowing something unwholesome. There's
no one but you to tell. But that's all right: my confidence in you
is absolute.

Zhou Yiyuan told me that his sister must meet me before
the next festival. Some taint in their community needed to be

cleansed. I listened yet couldn't follow him. He spat words from the side of his mouth as he spoke of greater and lesser generations. Ours was a lesser since our master was great and lesser generations nurtured great masters.

Because the villagers stare yet won't meet my eyes, and Zhou speaks in code, and the master has cast me out, and brief fevers still visit, my mind is in turmoil. These worries beg the memory of other shocks.

My aunt sent me to the shop for uncle's fags and a tin of cat food and I looked at pictures a long time by the magazine rack and when I got home she'd been electrocuted and rushed to the hospital and I never saw her again.

A physics teacher explained chaos by blowing cigarette smoke at the open window through which I saw a man thin as a signpost in shorts and nothing else sending lines of traffic left and right by flailing his arms until an old lorry took him in the midriff.

When I was sixteen and had more or less shed my accent, my mother drove me out of Vancouver and let me off by the side of the freeway and I stuck out a thumb and, ride by ride, travelled east along the Trans-Canada.

Breast Window

I dreamed I was in a boat, letting the current take me, and the river was flowing away from the sea, and I woke up ecstatic — so happy to have avoided the threat of evolution and heredity, to have found the river guilty of reversing its course.

I have a great number of dark moles on my arms and sides and back, more each year, and each is an ancestral eye looking out at the people in the valley. Each is a point and innocent. If I take off my robe the moles see Zhou Yiyuan. Cancer is the fear of seeing too much and doing too little. All my father's family died of cancer. Cancer tasks vulnerability with horrific patience.

Middle of the Breast

I can't think straight today. I lost my glasses and found it difficult to manage the details of the demonstration. I couldn't remember the day's point. Everyone waited while I stared at the point chart, then at the names, then at the expectant faces. I couldn't see and felt so tired. Elaboration of the deeper paths, though clear within my own body, seemed impossible. The monastery and its practices seemed remote. Any attempt at explanation fell short. I fell short. Am falling still, if not short, then asleep.

Root of the Breast

I remember waking up alone in a hotel room, standing at the window in the morning light. The building was perched on a cliff overlooking a Norwegian river town, three streets converging on a bridge, the river below chaotic with spray. I paid the bill and walked out into autumn, all that dirty sky, got into my car and started the engine, defrost on high, coffee on the dash, childish excitement at the journey ahead. A successful run had ended — Hamsun's *In the Grip of Life* — and I wanted to cross Europe by car. Goodbye to the cast the night before. Then hours and hours behind the wheel, heading out over mountain passes, through local weathers, limping through the rain on the deck of a ferry, still Blumenschøn, insecure and arrogant, pushing on through border crossings, past forests and lakes, following river meanders and skirting villages and towns. I'd stop only to buy coffee and a sandwich at a fuel stop, or to piss by the side of a desolate road, the car ticking like clockwork on the empty snaking highway, the first dry snowflakes falling on my shoulders. So travelling east again, stitching each morning to night. And by night I'd be gaunt and gormless in the car with only headlights to illuminate the physical world, the flaring lights of others to keep me company. And tomorrow, with dumb luck, would be the same.

Five snails on the path today. A monk with a long-handled broom must be careful to sweep around them. Let them have their pilgrimage undisturbed.

Not Contained

Resin has sealed the earlier pages of my work — I left it on a fresh-cut stump — just as I was deciding to read what I had written. The potential of the past is sealed with fresh sap. The exposed rings of the stump left a pattern that may be read, but not by me. The rings, let's say, the episodes, the days. The tree's dying wish to over-write human history.

Let me try this. The past is not worth figuring out — my life, my accomplishments, Shakespeare, Marlowe, Synge, Beckett, Handke, my rise and fall, my responses to theatre's roiling manifestations and joy then filmmaking's tedium and belly laughs. What happened yesterday, even the snails, is not worth present contemplation. There is music, a pulse, from the village by the river; geese honk overhead; rain falls so gently it doesn't stir the dry leaves of the willow. I will find a way to enter the centre of the village, to be accepted and acknowledged; the heart of that pulse was an empire a moment ago.

SUPPORTING FULLNESS

Let me try this. An ordinary working man barrowed compost from the pile to fertilise the field. Let's say the dirt, inadvertently carried from work to home, from relationship with cast and crew to relationship with a woman and child, had in it seeds to some important change. Let's say a dream told at work returns the favour, seeds internal change.

I think I understand Zhou Yiyuan. Certainly, I look forward to our next meeting. Meanwhile I keep my fingernails clean and bend over bodies to jar loose matter no heavier than the sum of my intangible parts.

Last night I was woken by the voice laughing then howling and yipping like a dog. It pulled me from sleep and I stepped outside. All dark, the soil wet, the trees dripping, though not from rain, from heavy dew. The other huts silent. The bathhouse steaming. Afraid, I could imagine the monks as orderlies and nurses. The master was a special doctor. The villagers were visiting their sick relatives. Who beside me was ill? Why was I so wide-awake? For the remainder of the night I stood listening to drops of dew falling from leaves onto the roof.

Season fire is over and season earth carries us toward metal. We will cut and carry wood for winter and the cooking fires. Listen. The yellow grass is hissing. I am dirt before the axe descends. Soon I will be water.

BEAM GATE

The morning bell in the day's third hour is a ceiling to sleep. A calling in of the living. The deer look up, their triangle faces all knowledge and care and strategy.

In my salad days, when the alarm woke me for theatre school it called me into loneliness. Folks under the pink sky at the bus stop were accidents. We paused in unison to light our cigarettes and nod good morning. Only accidents. I'd lose myself in roles, notes, affairs, then return home on the tube to further accidents and greater loneliness, a troubled sleep and fresh alarm. The electronic trill had to do with community, but also with authority. The pair that have confused and terrified me since the first day of kindergarten are now embodied in Zhou Yiyuan and Song Wei.

The blind bellringer, one of the oldest monks, lives in solitude near the spring above Mountain Temple. His bell hangs on a massive frame under a tile roof on an elevated piece of ground; it and North Shrine are the last edifices of our monastery complex before North Gate and the steps up the mountain. A short zigzag path leads from the bell mound down to the spring, then up to the gate. The blind monk teaches others how to use the bulldozer and the dump truck. He is good at small engine repairs and speaks rusty English since he lived several years in Evanston, Illinois, where he worked as a mechanic and met Thomas Cleary. He rings the morning bell when metal yin is fullest.

Today I was up and running to his hut before I was properly awake.

"I've fallen in love with one of the travellers!"

"Have you?"

"Yes."

"Does the master know?"

"The master has told me to follow her brother."

"Follow how?"

"Zhou Yiyuan is my new master."

The bellringer's shape moved back from his doorway. He sat on the floor. "I have never heard of this. Bring me some water."

I filled a cup from the barrel by the door and gave it to him. "You may come in and sit with me, but I can't help you."

This valley, the monks, the temple and shrines, the bamboo forest, the paths. Close my eyes and I'm living close to where I was born, on the banks of the Ribble in rural Lancashire, in a secluded asylum for people who can no longer cope with the discrepancy between their inner lives and the highly textured boxes into which the world has been sorted. As the doctors cross their lawn, we retreat into backwaters while our bodies run amok, amok, and have to be restrained with drugs and jackets, then pacified with elaborate illusions: now we are actors in a play; now we are monks studying the ancient eternal classics, each day woken by a bell rung by an old blind man who once spoke with Thomas Cleary, who says that he has in him a book of his own, who says he can't help me.

There is perfection in the idea of this being a dream, but when the old monk speaks to me in his rough American English of the birds in the valley, those that live by the river or on the mountainside or in the bamboo forest, how some he knew when he was a boy have disappeared, then I see that perfection does not have enough room. Perfection is not big enough. In the storehouse a room is always kept empty; it has dark corners and a trapdoor to the cellar and a sealed door to the granary.

My father and mother were born in Preston near the Ribble. My father lived in my grandfather's attic with my great grand-father's chest of tools. My dad was a diluted cabinetmaker with many physical skills and a talent for silence and absence. I'm a talking version of him. The old tools he left me I lost or sold.

Pass Gate

Everyone slept on his feet on the night journey to the sea. The start of fall, named for the squirrel, involves the expression of human sorrow for all life between sky and earth and a long walk to get news from the hermit monk.

"Wasps have invaded two shrine festivals and a temple ceremony," he told us. "Something is happening. Late Heaven is being rearranged. Wasps in great abundance."

And it was true. Even in lantern light wasps caught in our sleeves and danced drunk in our faces. Everyone was stung.

On the island we ran *Wei mo*, the Great Regulator.

(What is lost is lost in the great death or in one of the many minor deaths. My heart grieves for you. My heart grieves for all who have made way for me. My heart grieves for the mother of the drowned son. The laugh I hear from the river in the dead of night is a premonition of the arrival of the unknown. My heart grieves for the birds the old monk remembers from sixty years ago. Something *has* happened. A final curtain. A wrap. A book put down, finished with. A moment of hesitation and doubt.)

I lit lanterns on the posts around the island shrine to illuminate the four paths. Then I carried three lanterns to the three points of the island; at each location I had to wait until the place had forgotten me. Then I gathered the others and led them to the shrine.

Later, alone on the shore, sand squirming beneath my toes, the black-silver current twirling watery acres of twilight, I dug my fingers into the rich soil of the river plain; I thought I might bring something home to the temple, something precious from the time before our valley was inhabited. And hunched there, I saw our valley filled with rubble and fallen shrines and myself trying to climb through the detritus without sending the whole patchwork crashing in on itself. What d'you think? Is Song Wei the new Imogen? Is she the embodiment of all I have made way for?

Supreme Unity

When the alembics are unpacked from their cases and arranged for use and the hermit is consulted and the straw dogs burned and the blind bellringer's bobcat has smoothed the land behind West Shrine after burying the drainrock so the shrine won't flood this winter and the leaves have been swept away and we have gathered to hear the birds at sunset, last sun red and hot on our shoulders, our breaths held in unison, the actors take their places and the slow autumn dance begins. The monks and the villagers, complete, no one missing. The master and two priests are all that's needed to bridge heaven and earth; their movements and chants fill not only the vessels, but each fissure in the valley's mantle and every political hiatus in history with water as innocent of life as the first rain. We washed sea-salt from our feet. We salved our wasp stings. We prayed until we were all asleep.

Slippery Flesh Gate

Once through the great outer gate, a curved path runs north past the warrior tree, under the small gate, and then along a wooden walkway through the courtyard. Bow to the wishing tree and the well. This morning, walking to the storehouse, I came upon Zhou Yiyuan practising on the walkway. As he crouched, waves of heat rippled out from his belly and blew me back a step. Mountain Temple seemed to float in the air on the left shoulder of the storehouse. The mountain reared above the temple, its face brilliant in the sun. Zhou held his *qi* and I passed him quickly, shuddering, and forgot to bow to the wishing tree.

Rain was falling into the well, not real rain, but a kind of focused downpour of tiny red blossoms.

The storehouse is vast. Built of massive fireproof timbers five hundred years ago, it is the oldest building in the region and attracts more visitors than the temple, which is only two-hundred-and-sixty years old. When I entered the south door, the west side of the building was lost in shadows, and the tall windows high on the east wall were like the night buildings of a distant city. The great practice hall doubles as a drying room in winter. Time moves slowly here. The ceiling arches high overhead. The stairs, of black wood, lead to a railed walkway, to rooms and chambers where the belongings of the community are stored. In the lower northwest corner is the library. In the northeast corner of the groundfloor is the empty room.

After an hour of darkness and silence there, I blinked and returned; the red petal rain filled the doorway; it only faded when I walked through it and was outside again — the dwarf nowhere to be seen.

Calmer, I bowed to the mountain. Two late swallows were dipping and swooping above the temple's layered roofs. A building said to break the hearts of those who see it by moonlight covered in snow.

HEAVEN'S PIVOT

A slow passage into tidal disturbance is how I remember the end of life in Canada, physical energy rousing me only a few moments each day for the small film parts and theatre festival appearances that had all but vanished. A gradual turn northward out of Active Pass, final sun flashing on the water, seals rising from green depths, their silver-grey bodies streaming bubbles. *Who is passing above? What motors are stirring our world?*

I was on a ferry from Vancouver Island, having abandoned a short run in a small production (local troup, local playwright), glancing up from my computer screen. It was midwinter, my hand was bandaged, and I'd just received news of my ex-wife's death, and was absently clicking through a website dedicated to Asian village shrines.

Now I breathe and chant with other monks, and plunge once a season, oftener in summer, into the river below the mountain.

The sun burns hot. The day hangs fire. My heart rises at the scent of oil on my fingers, on the wooden shrine figures. All morning I stood or knelt beside bodies and felt the channels light up. As usual, hooded witnesses mildly curious about this work waited by my side, crosslegged watchers observing human-flavoured energy cycle and flare. Were you among them? I think you were.

A year ago I sat in the branches of the warrior tree and watched Imogen swaying from her hut with her luggage. Two monks accompanied her downhill to the river and over the bridge. I lost sight of her in the trees on the other side, but waited for the return of the monks. They came walking briskly — the morning was cool and mist lay on the water and on the banks — and were laughing together.

Next morning I lay sick on my mat and listened to the rain. I heard each drop hit the roof, roll down the tiles, fall through the air and hit the ground.

Zhou Yiyuan stood in the forest to one side of the path as I swept. Morning light streamed through the dying leaves of the plum trees. He skipped left and right on the balls of his feet and a shaft of sun lit his dark face. His eyes, when he looked up at me, sparkled. They were very black.

"You have not named a place. We have missed a festival. Meet my sister tonight on the bridge after the bell is struck, after the bus passes."

He was quiet a long time. A breeze moved here and there in the grasses and in the high branches above our heads.

"This is the moment," he said. "Otherwise conflict."

OUTER MOUND

This meeting fills me with excitement and dread. I count steps everywhere, breaths, leaves, geese, half up the mountain and back, then all the way to the river. I count monks, villagers, days, productions, appearances, lovers, cities, but no number will provide me with a clue to what will happen next.

She was waiting on the bridge already, the bus behind her, its windows shining through the trees, the engine loud until, with a huge wink, it shrieked into the night. Silence. A single frog croaking. A million crickets.

Song Wei held an electric lantern and was dressed in a tight-fitting silver shirt and silver trousers. Her dusky skin looked black in contrast to the shimmering bands of fabric. She turned and hurried across the bridge toward the road. Her light went out and she was cutting upriver along the south-bank trail before I gathered my wits and followed. She was a white blur, easy to make out under the thick river trees, her black hair swinging across her silver back, a supple crease. Her bare feet slapped the dry path.

Only after hearing car doors slamming did I register the sound of a motor being shut off on the road above. Footsteps and loose male laughter. A geometric tangle of light beams descending.

The gang swept through drifts of leaves to arrive on the trail ahead of me and flowed like a wave toward the woman, who dropped her lantern, raised a hand. Flashlights converged on her and the moment was as fluid as mercury.

Wind in high branches and the low gurgle of the river.

They surged along the path. Some I knew from the settlement; others were strangers. I recognised Zhou's squat form. Song Wei gave a sharp cry and was caught by the first to reach her, a boy and two men, who dragged her to a fallen tree.

It was an old scene, an often-repeated set of actions, an eternal secret vile code that I possessed the capacity for witnessing, though this was not the night-scene of a black-and-white film. Now I charge myself with what I saw, but at the time I did nothing except pay attention.

"Here is the extinction of luck," her brother told me early this morning when we were shivering on the beach, the fire between us dead.

"What does that mean?" I said.

"An ancient remedy," he said. "A boundary skirmish."

"I don't understand," I said.

The bell sounded from across the river to signal the beginning of the new day.

"What a terrible thing!" I said.

The Great

And then night, sleep and dreams; blame drunkenness for all, all the men were drunk and losing control, of their bodies, then restraints — forget work, forget colleagues, forget rules, morning will never come — forget ethics, order, reason.

An inverse ratio: to the extent that our boundaries are weak, our exertion of control must be strong. Comes the declaration of war and the first battle plans. Do I know what I'm talking about? Rape as a setting of limits — a terrible thing. Nothing here makes the kind of sense I was educated to perceive. The village at night is full of turtles and fish; in every hut they swim, small and big, all colours, while people hang onto their bottles and continue to drink. I am with my father who falls into machinery when crossing a swingbridge. I meet an old friend whose face is dear to me, and an enemy, sober, who says the boat is sinking and suggests we swim home. "You are doing this all wrong," he says. "You will never find your way if you go farther in that direction." And my sister gives me a pet bug: a small praying mantis that immediately escapes its box.

A bedtime game I played with my son: "Here's writing on your back, writing on your chest, writing on your arms and legs, and on your fingers and on your toes. Now climb into your envelope. Here's a kiss for a stamp. Now let's mail you to dreamland. Think of where you want to be. Night-night, off you go."

Say it is research into causes, the work I am doing, and these are not monks and villagers (not inmates either), but players, and I write lines each night for them to perform next day, not knowing completely what I'm doing. What will happen at dawn? What will the river carry down or the road transport to our gate? I'm not confident that the events of tomorrow will fit well with the events of yesterday. The lines, the lines. We need to meet the lines anyway, meet them halfway, as they come, because if we don't then this valley will lose its witness and will not know itself. Say all this is so, my father and mother dead, my wife dead and our son gone, I may have had to cast myself out. West is the usual heading, aiming for a complete revolution.

First thing today I went to see Song Wei and her brother, without expecting to find them. But they were both there. She seemed shy and unhurt, her face pure and open. Confused, I told them I had no power in this community, no voice, that I was like them, an outsider, and from a culture that to almost everyone else in the valley was a dream, whereas this — and I waved my arm wildly — for me this was the dream. They did not seem interested. Zhou Yiyuan began at once to petition for my help. He knew I would help them now to gain favour with the master of the monastery.

"How can I act after what happened last night?" I said.

Zhou raised his eyebrows. He rubbed his hands together. He said he'd noticed that the timbers of the bridge were beginning to show signs of decay from exposure to the rain and wind and sun, and he would like to offer his services in undertaking to repair the bridge before winter, the present season being suitable, with the low level of the river and the warm dry days and, if agreed upon, he and his workers could begin at once.

The formal rehearsed nature of this speech was terrifying. His chin jutted toward Song Wei. I saw her body arched across the dead tree, the men circling.

"He has told me that you are my new master," I said.

He leered at me, his head weaving like a cobra. "Tell him," he said to his sister.

She turned slowly, then stared into my eyes. "We build a box in autumn, fill it through winter."

A long gleaming golden strand from her eyes hooked a sibling strand in mine and some plan, some shape materialised. Such forms as this are usually kept underground and are only hinted at in myth or brought out in performance. I know this because

I've been in love. I've acted out of love. But I'm in a different land. These are forms I do not understand.

RETURN

Today we planted pines beside South River Shrine. Great Central Channel represented in saplings. We carried water in buckets from the river, one per tree. We sang to each tree beginning with Wind Palace. For some reason, by the end I was weeping like a child. I fell to my knees and when I looked up everyone was standing, head bowed, everyone but the master, who was looking at me with a smile. I've never seen trees so tame and helpless or a sky so blue. Each needle glinting, isolate. The circle and silence were in service to every aspect and absence of aspect this side of art. Here was beauty again.

Then Zhou Yiyuan walked into our midst with his own bucket and set it at my feet. There was an intake of breath. Even though I've put it away, I still recognise stagecraft. My face in the bucket of water was a shock.

RUSHING QI

This is the last day of the month and the hour of kidney, opposite to heart, fire burning on water. Zhou dozes head down outside the shrine while I write. He has brought me a black box, heavily ornamented, indicating that I am to give it to the master for the temple. The box smells smoky. It sits to one side of the folding desk, at the edge of the shrine deck.

As the day closes, the master appears at the end of the path and pauses to lean on his stick.

Zhou wakes and gazes at the master, then gets to his feet and backs into the bamboo.

After dark I went to the master's hut. He received the box with a bow. When I spoke Zhou Yiyuan's name, he raised his voice and declared that the bridgework would begin in the morning. He announced that all the monks would sleep under the stars tonight to celebrate 9/9 of the yin calendar.

Fog rolled in and I slipped through the forest downhill to the river. The nomads sat around their fires and barely stirred as I wavered there, out of breath, and Song Wei came forward to take my hand. We found a path into the heavy wild land. No one came here, only animals.

The night fog continued to roll in and the leaves, fat with water, dripped on us as we lay together in the bamboo forest. I woke once in the night. Song Wei slept on her back. I watched her, then set my shoulders into the soft earth. We were side by side, facing the sky. It felt as though stars were bursting on my eyes.

At the morning bell, I crawled to the warrior tree and prayed, then joined the monks in the storehouse courtyard between the well and the wishing tree. Our bodies were soaked from the dripping leaves, our eyes fresh from sleep. We ran through silken movements, then into the storehouse and lit the braziers.

October

Thigh Gate

AND SO THERE IS INDUSTRY ON THE BANKS, a new frenzy of
hammering, and men splash around the pilings, calling to one
another, while grassfires burn along the river. We all know the
end of fine weather spells the beginning of winter.

When Imogen was an adolescent I was a young man, newly
married. Five years ago she was exploring the river by boat,
naked under her white dress, the sun low in the sky, stepping
onto the dock, the dark trees a backdrop, a simple fabric scrim.
An accidental breeze the main character. The monks laughing
and dipping their eyes.

The dark ornate box was open on the floor of the master's
room, a long yellow swatch of silk spilling from the charred
inside into the shadows under the single window. An evening
bird sang from a near branch.

The master said he wanted a small group of monks to go to
three cities to meet physicians and journalists and give a demonstration of our practice, and to consult a woman prophet.

"I have a story," I said.

"Tell your new master." He poured hot water and prepared tea. He passed me a small green steaming cup. "You will go."

Crouching Rabbit

The point is a small hole where something precious is buried. The rape I witnessed is a bucket I have yet to set down. When I approach the details my mind sheers away. I can remember only the feel of Song Wei's dusky skin. Only her eyes.

Early this morning, for the first time in a while, came the scream of the madman across the valley, and at dawn Zhou and his sister crossed the bridge, each carrying a small bundle and a lantern. The village watchman told the headman of the field party and he told me.

Yin Market

When the bell rang I realised I must talk to the bellringer. I left the shelter of the trees. The master was in the middle of the bridge casting something away, shaking a bag, container, vessel. Something wiggled free. Hemming him in were the idle crane and the empty scaffolding. The bridge repairs, barely begun, have been halted. No work yesterday or today. I hurried uphill to the knoll where the blind monk lived, feeling too close to the wind, the clouds, afternoon birds, the smell of apples, the last berries on the vine.

"Fall is here," I said.

"It isn't, not yet," said the bellringer.

"The brother and sister have gone. The master — "

"You have disturbed me. Go away."

I turned and retraced my path. The sun was out and the birds sang madly.

Beam Hill

Last night a large deer craned his neck into the window of my hut. Antlers and stars, the half-moon behind. Even when I sat up, he did not withdraw. He huffed. A doe waited in the grass by the edge of the plum border.

The idea of leaving the valley, even for a short time, is frightening. I'm not ready to represent anything or anyone, not even myself, and not the single-point treatment, the spontaneous analysis, the deep assessment. I'm also unprepared for restaurants and shops and taxis, noise and crowds and the stink of traffic.

During my first years here I was calm. The phone had stopped ringing; the computer had faded. Now I am agitated. Song Wei has gone. I can't even focus on Imogen. What a lot of work to develop that story: her boyish testiness, her lanky goofy beauty. Chaplin's girl directed by Chaplin himself — that selfish, that fragile, that certain. Ah, but Song Wei tasted of north.

Calf's Nose

Away across the river to the bus and then dozing through the forest with a briefcase of letters, freezing cold, my fingers chilled, the afternoon nearly done, on our way not to find the prophet or demonstrate the power of the Great Point, but to convince the dwarf to return. The master angry with me, the floor gritty underfoot, the engine's revving astoundingly desolate. A cloud mass seethed across the sky. No stars. No stars, no direction.

We stepped down at midnight, trembling, at the coastal town on the outskirts of the port and walked icy streets to the small monastery where we warmed ourselves with food and then ran the day's path along each other's bodies.

In sex and thoughts of sex I return to a small place in myself, a fissure in the ground at CV-6 say, and follow the blue in my forearms and wrists. This blood opens on a secret river.

Leg Three Miles

I hold Stomach-36, lower Sea of *Qi*, and CV-6, Sea of *Qi*.

Hello *Dantian*, Lower Cinnabar Field, yang point to tonify the kidneys, junior relative of *Guan Yuan* the yin gate of origin! Are you indicating *qi* deficiency of my fire *zang*? I hereby option original *qi*, dynamic *qi* dancing between the kidneys. I hereby promote pre-heaven *qi* to foster post-heaven *qi* of the earth. I hereby address the foundation of human life and all *qi* deficiency and the exhaustion of anything! The image is of this guy digging a hole long and deep enough to lie in.

Zhou Yiyuan and his sister are well known here, an illustrious pair. Those we spoke to told us he was headman of a revolutionary gang and she a shaman from the mountains; they are outlaws. They show up most years in autumn, usually with a group of followers.

We found him drinking tea with merchants in a market alley, the day bright and warm, his sister weaving with a group of women several feet away. We reminded him of his promise to mend the bridge and he shrugged. "Am I your master?"

"Yes."

"You wish me to return?"

"Yes."

"You will lose everything."

The merchants sipped milky black tea and laughed; Song Wei and I stared at each other; my brother monk was smiling, while hawkers with cages and carts bustled around us. The air a fizz of ecstatic flies. Parrots and pigs seemed related.

Upper Great Void

I can't see these words clearly and the words are not only smaller but they dance about. The night is cold. Numb fingers mean the words, smaller and dancing, come slower. I wish I could say the same for thoughts. Once upon a time and not so long ago thoughts came one by one and I woke before dawn to watch them trot around a track, the sense of control rising till I rose. Then I got within range of the little thoughts coughing in the dust of the big ones and here was the first of all lessons — don't slow down or you'll get lost in details. Every enterprise is an exponential whirligig. Speed keeps everything trim. You are safe and fluid as long as you increase.

Those were happy people at the marketplace, at the cusp of increase and deficit. Zhou Yiyuan was loquacious. Of course he would return to finish the job he began. Wasn't he the heart of the work force? Without him real work could not begin. The bridge would collapse without him. The machinery would seize, the crews disband. He bought wine for his friends and stumbled drunk from one side of the alley to the other. Now did we understand? Now did we see how essential he and his people were?

I gave up trying to listen and set my eyes on Song Wei's bright grace. The raw yarn running through her quick fingers was white and red.

Lines Opening

The Great Point is the one that when released will set all in order. Spontaneous analysis or deep assessment will find this point. The trick is to know which approach to use. The full moon is on the wane and the sky bright with stars. Listen. On a similar night I walked along another alley, familiar and dusty, junk to either side, past the shuttered guitar shop, with my wife and son. I'm not trying to fool you. You're the one thing I can't lose.

LOWER GREAT HOLLOW

Imogen came to me in the night, younger than I had ever seen her, younger even than in her early films, carrying a feverish baby. We were inside a shadowy barn or stable and the baby was starving and we had to chew bread to moisten it . . . the little mouth opened . . .

This morning I couldn't find my broom. The broom was not in its place. Hard to credit the size of emotion this loss engendered. I felt such pity for the broom, which I remembered as a new thing with fresh stalks of young bamboo, green and flexible, tied with red twine to a straight smooth yellow wood handle. I was given it shortly after my arrival, and we have been together these long years and cleared the paths season after season and have grown old together. My fingers oiled the shaft each fall. The bristles were thinning, but still.

I have searched the forest and the ground beneath each tree. Someone has taken the broom while I was away. Zhou Yiyuan has returned already and taken it, perhaps, because it is mine. Now I'm afraid of losing everything, as he said I would.

All I've collected since the foundation of the world. Things I hid since God was a boy. Things I've forgotten. All reformations.

Brooms, of course. House brooms, outside brooms.

ABUNDANT BULGE

Two gunshots from the forest to the west. These, together with bits of news filtering in from the outside world, make Zhou Yiyuan's prophecy believable. Sunshine on wet unmown field grass, webs woven by night heavy with dew — all fragile, on their way out. The dew almost frost.

Chosŏn detonated an atomic bomb in a cave. The princely stag that passed me going west an hour ago may be already dead. The repair crew seems agitated as Zhou Yiyuan strides from the frantic encampment to the bridge and back. He's preparing his people to move on, to finish or give up on the bridge. We hear they are under threat from another tribe.

To the southwest a dog has been barking since I began writing ten minutes ago. The gunshots and the dog are probably related. Sunlight fixes the great chestnut to its massive crown of exposed roots. The trunk towers over the roof of the shrine and the ground is littered with shiny nuts and split green casings. I hear steps in the leaves.

Stream Divide

Yesterday Zhou Yiyuan brought a sealed message from his sister, placed it on the ground, bowed, then stepped from the shrine back into the shadow of the tree.

Will you claim the child?

A channel opens between their village and the monastery, actions from my past waiting to erupt, but to what purpose? What chance would my old sperm have against that of the rampaging boys and men?

This morning there was a small earthquake. Then I found my broom on the ground: I had left it in a tree, between two sets of forked branches.

Rushing Yang

The master summoned me to his hut near the wishing tree. He was sitting in the courtyard on a red carpet amid fallen leaves and held the black box. We gazed at each other and listened to the birds.

"An earthquake shook the temple," he said. "Was that you?"

"No, Master."

"I am not that for you."

"I would like to stay here," I said.

He cocked his head to one side. "Before going to the cities, I want the three of you to carry an offering over the mountain. Fill your bags with the best fruit and grains and the finest honey and take them to North Valley."

We left at midnight and travelled by half-moon along the dry path where our sweat froze along *Du Mai* and our arms ached.

At dawn we stopped to eat some of the fruit, my idea, and then continued our climb. Bamboo gave way to pines, dark and velvet, night flickering beneath their branches even at midday.

My two companions slept in a circle of massive rocks. I was too cold and tired to understand the meaning of this task or of any dreams or thoughts or words, but I still unfolded the little desk. My child is in the past not the future. I can't think what I'm supposed to learn from Zhou Yiyuan, nor from the master who keeps sending me away. My limbs ache and my sinuses are clogged. I'm colder than I've ever been. This place is lost in white fog, the setting sun a great yellow primitive eye.

Was the central pavilion of my life a theatre, a shrine, or a forest hut? I remember the night my wife gave birth to our child. Such an entanglement of love and worry and release. Her face against the pillow and his arrival.

We made fire and warmed our hands, breathing clouds of mist, listening to near-human cries: out of the milk-white sea came a small herd of cattle.

I loved the unnamed world. I emptied hope of its contents and still it haunts its old environs, slack as a spent purse, looking for some grains of dust and a couple of thin seeds. I have in my pocket a letter to give to the abbot at North Valley Monastery and have promised to bring back a reply.

SUNKEN VALLEY

A grey dog joined our party and led us west. My brother monks have travelled this way before, so their judgement was quick when the path forked; they agreed with the dog. The dog, they said, must be a North Valley dog, from one of the villages, and would lead us to the nearest pass. But the dog, though happy to be with us, did not seem trustworthy to me.

On Snow Pass the wind was blowing. The others practised English with me as we walked. I thought we were lost, but one said if we descended more or less north then we would reach a road and soon one of the villages. The other said we should be farther east and might — it was possible — miss the villages if we turned north, but if we went east would no doubt come to a marker or shrine. "The dog is a very good sign," he said. "Certainly a sign from which to take our direction."

INNER COURTYARD

Rain. At first rain was in the air but not falling. Then it began. We were still wandering the narrow defile at the summit and had found no marker. And then the dog ran off among the rocks. The rain fell hard and soon turned to sleet. Our journey was in ribbons. Top Pass was hidden. The only thing we agreed on was that whatever pass we eventually did find would not be the traditional one between the two valleys. The dog was gone.

A slash of sleet. What it chose to fall on. Where it struck skin, earth. Blame was everywhere. I couldn't distinguish cause from blame.

We blundered steadily on all day and then found shelter beneath an overhanging rock, and slept in the fading afternoon light, trusting snow wouldn't bury us.

Harsh Mouth

Lost. We heard barking again; in the pitch-black distance it was a welcome sound. We peered out at the feeble light. We were soaked and freezing in the cave and we huddled together under the dripping roof and dozed, flakes dancing outside.

A leopard crossed in front of our eyes, its tracks filling instantly with snow. The cat stopped, sniffed the air, stared across the path at us, crouched in our shallow cave. *Blood warmer.* Such desolation between us, then static, *qi* fizzing, all our hackles reared.

Hidden White   # Yin Earth

ALL NIGHT PRAYERS. AN ANIMAL SCREAMING. SMALL FIRE from the last of our stash of wood. Small intestine. Then stars.

We left rice and fruit for the leopard. Smoke rose to our right as we turned north and began to descend a clear path. The leopard had not eaten us. We trudged down through the snow. Opened the outer frontier gate. *Waiguan.* Triple Warmer *luo.*

GREAT METROPOLIS

We laboured along the path from Leopard Pass for half a day before we came to this forest clearing, where the buildings and the birds seemed familiar, though the people spoke in a strange dialect. Many of them were sick. There had been waves of illness during the past year. Nothing was certain, they said. Routine was washed away.

"Our seasons are disordered!"

"Old streams have run dry!"

"Our best well has failed completely!"

"Is your winter coming too soon as well?"

We exchanged news with the elders and the others went to sleep while I waited in a cold outbuilding for the abbot to send for me. It took an hour to dry my paper in front of the tiny fire.

I want to go home to River Mountain as soon as possible — tomorrow if the weather is fine. Fear has tightened the faces of these people. Snow clouds are rolling in, and wind gusts on the high slopes. It's early for such cold, and if we stay longer the mountain may become too difficult to cross.

SUPREME WHITE

"Are you out of the fray or part of the fray?"

GRANDFATHER GRANDSON (YELLOW EMPEROR)

I could not answer the North Valley abbot. He had kept us waiting two days, then sent word late last night. I gave him the letter and the fruit and honey and we sat together in the light from an oil lamp while an owl hooted every half-minute as he wrote. He sealed his letter and gave it to me. He said he would visit River Mountain next summer — the world would be changed by then. Then he asked his question. It was freezing in his room and my teeth were chattering.

Later I thought of what to say, when we'd climbed through the pass again and were on our way down toward the river, which we saw through holes in the clouds.

I was squatting behind a large double-trunked maple and an owl as calm as Buddha was blinking at me from a branch. "The fray is ahead. The fray is behind. I'm not part of the fray." I retied my clothes and returned to my companions and told them. They smiled and nodded.

Once out of the snow we made camp. We ate and prayed. We discussed the dog and the leopard and what else winter might bring. Clouds rolled through the forest and the sun came out. We felt warm in the arid spicy smell of crumbling yellow leaves.

SHANG HILL

We chased, leaping, toward home. We saw the temple roof at first light. Opened the gate quietly. Not ghosts returned to haunt, but adventurers with stories. Prodigals practiced at the leopard's prowl and the owl's smooth turn.

THREE YIN CROSSING

Before the story is made up it's perfect. Each telling spoils it. Now we must take down the cave shrine. The master himself came to watch. He stood head bowed, each hand warming itself in the opposite sleeve, very still, while the sun shone on the massive green timbers. The shrine in the cave looked impossible from every perspective. Impossible to build, impossible to dismantle. Too ancient, too holy. And yet when we pulled gently at the wood, fitting our fingers into the chinks between the rock face and the structure, it fell into pieces at our feet. Nothing has been keeping it together, though monks have bought their dead masters to this shrine for hundreds of years. The cave looked meek and toothless now, the ground in front worn smooth, the sun shining on a raised ridge of bird shit beneath where the roof-edge had been. The master turned away.

DRIPPING VALLEY

I used to drink coffee, which fed a deep sense of anticipation, heart fire. These days are like that, full of expectation, Indian summer boosting the nerves and sunshine in the valley every day. The villagers' voices grow louder, though they seem less agitated. The bridgework is progressing after all.

Mornings are thick with fog that soon burns off, trees dripping dew onto yellow and red leaves. Sadness, though, accompanies earth. It will soon be the season of metal, grandfather of wood and spring, time to release grief. Then winter, fire's grandmother: the Great. Here, unlike North Valley, the seasons are still ordered.

Every night I dream of cities. I've already been displaced twice this month. I still do not want the responsibility of transmitting or translating our knowledge.

"I don't want another journey," I said to the master.

"And yet you will go and meet these physicians and masters. You will see the prophet."

"I don't want to leave the valley."

"It's only an aspect of yourself leaving."

I have the intimation of something, yet it feels like memory: a specific memory, something that happened to me, a happy thing; the light in my wife's eyes when we were very close, before it all fell apart and I left and she got sick.

Once we were in the woods, I remember. We'd walked a short distance from the country road into the ferns and firs of a sunny hillside. We were on the soft ground and I was on top of her. We were unexplored then, and the light in her eyes was a new reflection of blue sky, her eyes themselves the colour of earth. So this intimation has to do with that moment.

Last night the master raised his head and let me see his face. We had finished our sessions for the day. I'd felt his presence as I worked — gall bladder, following metal and water along the great central channel, my partner's body releasing in a series of muscle spasms — and after bowing at the session's end, I turned. The master let his hood fall back and his face was open in the dim light, eyes full of tears.

I can't believe this world has other countries, lovers, other shocks and deaths and thoughtless blunders. At prayer, just now, my knees were screaming with pain and the small of my back ached, so that I could concentrate on nothing else, and time slowed until all meaning, all responsibility fled my consciousness. The other voices went on, but I heard mine skip syllables and stop.

Something is coming out of the future and all I can imagine belongs to the past. The master's tears. The ridge of bird shit. The fist of rice on the snow.

The last time I saw my wife was in the hospital. No, not that moment. Later, on the city bus, going home after she'd died. Hollowed out. Some words spoken behind my back: "He would like to canoe down the Mississippi." An old woman across the aisle eating a tomato in a fastidious, slightly ashamed way, eating it like an apple, her head nodding, a book half-closed in her free hand.

Why have I kept such a thing all this time? And the seals in Active Pass. And we even had a child, a boy, and mine and loved by me. And you who read this. Who are you anyway? How and why did you happen?

Yin Mound Spring

The temple, the cave, East Shrine and West Shrine, South River Shrine, the lesser shrines, all the paths between. I am in dread of the bridge because I will cross it soon and fly away and perhaps never return.

Heavy frost this morning. The temperature is falling every day. The village is diminishing, its inhabitants going off, one by one or in small groups. Their enemy invisible, if one even exists. Now the bridgework is almost finished only a few families remain.

All the day's light is focussed on the tops of trees, birds singing last songs. A couple of frogs spoke a moment ago. I heard this afternoon a whisper in my partner's lung — we both heard it as we released his large intestine channel. We both knew it was the whisper of a shadow.

I've taken to reading by the well afternoons when the weather is clear, on the small seat there, reading from old texts. From there I can see through the two gates to the warrior tree, which has lost nearly all its leaves.

Sea of Blood

Lonely, today. I have not seen Song Wei since returning from North Valley. A day of rain and at every prayer and chant I fall asleep. Meditation is sleep. The bell is sleep. I hold onto nothing else. The forest teems with yearnings for hibernation. Let the snows fall. The cave is empty, its last miner dust, its last master crumbled. Let me take their place and sleep all winter.

Dustpan Gate

Each season is an enclosure, each month, each day and each moment separate. I hated leaving the valley, yet I loved being on the mountain. I always hated performance, yet loved rehearsal. I bought my lucky leather jacket in London. It was thin and beautiful, scarred and lined with scruffy wool and I kept it on a hook beside the doctors' photograph. The people over the pass, pale and disturbed by illness, were envious of us. The abbot, who will visit us next summer when the world is different, may steal something. What has he told the master?

The turning of a page. That sound. The page turning, the whisper of millennia this side of history. Pages turning and the hiss of brush or scratch of pen or quill, ownership and mystery on speaking terms. Monks have always sat hunched and shivering with cold while they copied the contents of some vision, startled by a door crashing, invaders on horseback, but so embarked and hungry that even as boots echo in the halls, they hold to their squinty path between laziness and passion.

It would take only a single well-armed man to hold Leopard Pass. This thought arises because I'm afraid of losing what might already be lost.

What value have I for the world? Today I practiced in the forest, alone except for the wind and twirling leaves and didn't want the day to gather darkness, but it did.

Rushing Gate

It sounds dry, the page turning in a room, thumb and forefinger of the left hand rubbing the page to make certain of a single leaf. When the thumb pulls up two or more pages the sound is large and chaos threatens. The creak and kink of the page, so pleased to be turned, separates two faces that have been nose to nose in obscurity for years, even centuries. Perhaps it's the first time they have been apart or the last time they will be separated. They lie flat, gazing at the ceiling, stunned by light and solitude, and as suddenly as life began it is over and they're plunged into darkness, dark word to dark word, every page trapped, the boards shut, one book in a shelf of books.

Do I miss you? Yes I do. Turn the page. Do I miss you? Still yes. Turn a new leaf. Let's see what I can imagine.

Turning seventy. Going away. Unseen.

Abode of the Fu

Out with the tribe, I would have said, talked about this and that over croissants and espresso. About theatre and ambition, what we have and haven't done, how to advertise ourselves so we may survive a little way into the future. No.

I wanted to see Song Wei — afraid she might have been cast out — so left my digging in the field to go down to the river.

She sat on a rock, legs wide, pots in a circle on the gravel around her, her sleeves pinned back. The river noise masked my approach and she jumped when I called out. She was washing pots, her hair loose to her waist, a black curtain against the yellow robe, wet at the tips. Almost immediately her brother came over and crouched at her side and looked up at me. Sly gargoyle blink and grin.

ABDOMEN KNOT

"No names," said the master. "No names for the channels or the points." He studied the edge of his robe. Dust furred the folds. He turned to me. "That woman will show you a change of course. A new direction." He shook his head. Thin wisps of hair moved in the icy breeze. "Ah, it's cold today," he said. "It was warm yesterday."

"I do not wish to go on a journey."

The two other monks, my brother travellers, were still, their heads bowed. Even with three braziers burning in front of the statue, the wind penetrated. The master's face was half in shadow, the lit part serene, the dark part anxious. This would be our last meeting before we left.

When he cleared his throat we looked up. "Go to the river," he said. "Consult the River Map."

I lay on a mat. My partner chased *qi* along the tributaries of my body. Fire, earth, water — his fingers guiding me down. The smell of apples cooking, apples and rice. When I woke (it is always like waking, getting up from the mat) it was already dark, the path to my cold hut marked by a deep drift of yellow leaves.

GREAT HORIZONTAL

When we read the river map yesterday, Song Wei was performing a ritual on the bank. I paid more attention to her arms rising and falling than to the dripping knots. Then half a moon last night and a storm, so many swooping leaves that sunrise vanished in gold fractions, no sooner swept into piles than lifted in whirlwinds. One spun across the bridge toward the far shore, another twirled in the storehouse courtyard.

A child shouted, "Uh! Uh!" every time a family staggered over the bridge into the monastery grounds. The families that left have been returning all day. Has Song Wei made it possible for them to come back? Did they run into trouble?

Each day we see farther into the death cave now the sun is low and the shrine has been taken down, each day farther, as far as light will penetrate. And since the entrance faces southwest, evening gives us particles of light dancing where shadow begins — and beyond that?

ABDOMEN SORROW

Words are names or parts of a name, and because we cannot name, I sit with my folding desk by the shore of this pond and name.

Once part of the river and since split off, this pond is the temenos of the heron now, and heron stands in a reed-room, neck parallel with the water's surface. He is blue-grey and leaning toward fish in a sway begun centuries ago. When he is roused by the bell from his hunting to this page, I myself am abruptly split off from the putter of ducks in the pond into a dream so large its edges overlap with sky as I furnish the dream with labels.

I remember Imogen walking slowly around this pond, the reeds light yellow, olive green, dying; new shoots waiting in the bank, in the silt of the soft bank.

The low west sun warms my right cheek though all else is freezing. What's next? Building a stone tower and living inside its walls, finding a friend, cutting down a forest, renovating a cave, eating all the honey, revisiting my birthplace, listening to children?

Mountain is cut close to the blue sky. A warrior lights briefly on the bridge and his armour clangs like a bell.

Then Zhou Yiyuan is crouched beside me. He reaches into his robe and pulls out something wrapped in cloth. His breath smells of metal. He places on the ground a small wood carving. I am still writing, only vaguely aware of the heron walking on water, making an exit across the mud shallows, a writhing glossy snake in his beak. The ducks applauding.

November

Food Cavity

TODAY WAS SPENT CUTTING DOWN TREES with a howling chainsaw in a blue-grey fog, chips flying, then loading wood, three of us, into the truck bed, rear wheels axle-deep in mud, air stinking of gasoline and shattered branches.

Fell asleep at meditation.

The master has been low these past few weeks. We travelling monks are still parsing the knotted strings pulled from the river.

Sky Ravine

The appearance of a wisp of smoke sent me into the rain and uphill to the walled garden. Just north, near an old mineshaft, I disturbed Zhou Yiyuan. He trundled into the rocky woods, furious, his figure crashing into a tree, and quail flew up from the tangled grass. The remains of a corner-field ritual hissed at the northeast angle of the high wall. I ran to him and he caught my arm, pulled me to the ground and held me, his chest against mine.

"What are you doing?" I said.

We rolled in the grass. "Your child," he hissed, his lips close to my ear. Then he was up and away.

I walked back to the charred effects wet with rain still smouldering on a flat rock. Just burnt wood. Nothing human.

CHEST VILLAGE

So much rain in the past few days that a whole section of hillside collapsed when a small number of us were at East Shrine, soil and sand slipping around us, a horrible noise of splintering timbers. I died in the slide and haunted the village by the river.

ENCIRCLING GLORY

Wind and rain have invaded the valley. All the paths are mud and all the shrines dark and dripping. Smoke drifts above the river from the tents and shelters, and from our own numerous fires. We have turned on the electric lights. The master slipped and fell. He cracked his head on the frame of the storehouse door and is now lying in his room, flat on his back with his eyes open. Death seems close, if not his then someone's. The death of something. The village, the monastery, you. I'm counting again.

GREAT WRAPPING

Perhaps the world is dying. Until dawn we prayed in the northeast corners of each field and then the master appeared for the Dragon Festival, though he could not turn his head and seemed more than usually distracted and forgetful. The dragon set sail on the river but got so wet and heavy that her wing caught in a bare willow and she was dragged into the fast current. Several villagers waded in to rescue her and were carried downstream and had in turn to be rescued with bamboo poles. She was last seen flailing in rapids, approaching the gorge. The bits and pieces torn from her before she vanished have yet to be divined. We stood along the bank in our ceremonial robes. One sign was water-supporting-fire — the dragon's kidney — for me, I suppose, since I dredged it from the brown cataract.

The master's voice cracked like a whip. "Can anyone read this?" Then he fell again, unconscious, his robes flapping in the mud. The morning's blue sky gone in angry cloud; then rain, torrents, a dark deluge.

We stood by the master's bed. Winds slashed at the roof. The dragon was in the room with us, torn and deflated. This life makes us lonely, not storms. The air smelled of mould and sweat and wet cloth. It was impossible to keep him dry. We stood in a circle, shoulder to shoulder. The corner of a shoulder is a metal perch. *Jian Yu*. Shoulder bone. The knotted branch of a tree. Now we're lost who will lead us? We'll need a boat, an ark, for when our feet no longer touch the ground.

The master cleared his throat and nodded. He reached one arm in the air. "I know this place, yet it's different. Only a bend in the path where I hurt myself. I wonder what comes next?"

Summit Spring   Yin Fire

Like the weather with its successions of storms, each ripping then drenching the forest, stirring the river into a brown hissing snake wider every day, I am unsettled. I have always been change-resistant.

A day of rain and sutras and I'm a spineless grub waiting in its hole gazing fearfully up at the dirty sky, letting storms, winds, even a breeze, determine my course and saying that it was my talent, my gift, while in fact all has erupted willy-nilly, helter-skelter. Rain beats on the shrine roof. Thoughts crawl around with effortless patience and many reversals and repetitions, and only a connoisseur or a mother could appreciate their ugly little faces as they slither over the rough rich humus of a springtime garden, this very one in my head, nibbling a button here, a thread there, the sun a dimple, flowers smiles, toward some unthinkable end, meanwhile basking, each squirm exquisite, on a knee, a cheek.

Something you would appreciate, maybe: the way, between bouts of storm, thin foggy veils of cloud chase through the stands of bamboo. I watched clouds cross the river this morning, then walked to the bridge during a gap in the rain — everything shining, grey and silver — and looked back at the mountain, the top quarter lost in white, tendrils and fringes of cloud like the ghosts of fleeing children.

And while looking at the sky a thing occurred to me and I scurried back to the practice hall and worked in a dream as the thing expanded and developed its little politic. I had no course to abandon, no innocence to spoil. Imogen had managed to carry her innocence into adulthood and wore it now as a kind of thinness. Song Wei was a slender woman, pure and direct, her slight body powerfully grounded in this soil. My thinness was threshed wheat, done and dusty. I guess I have always gauged women according to an ancient hidden scale, and found them superior to me. Ah God, not my mother, please.

Men ± what? = women.

[89]

The answer will pierce my heart or pierce my kidneys. The final equation will decide the fate of the world. *Calm, calm.*

A stinging sleet fell on me as I walked deliberately from the storehouse to the temple.

CYAN SPIRIT

After the rain everything is simpler. The river has overflowed its banks and become a long wide lake on which ducks are already fishing. Winter is official. Many villagers have moved in with us since their dwellings are threatened. Children are everywhere; there must be dozens of them. Women turn up in surprising places, nearly always in an attitude of prayer. The men are surly and keep to themselves, in small groups, their black eyes scanning the monastery land.

This afternoon I served Zhou Yiyuan and the master tea in the master's hut. A small smoke-blackened wooden figure sat on the low lacquered table. Homunculus? Good grief, Song Wei's rape has married our two communities.

So, a lake. Abandoned shacks. With the long grass beaten down the earth seems small and shabby. All the nests I made have gone or have been squashed into absurd shapes, the way all human products fail when our pride meets the elements. So, simpler.

LESSER SEA

I heated water, prepared the tea, set bowls of rice on the little table between the men. Each head bowed a fraction. Wet leaves smouldering outside. Smell of burning pine needles, sweet, wafting from the fire.

Didn't we love pubs on winter afternoons, to go from the living day to the gloom and beery fug of a barroom? We were innocent then; we were boys and girls, and not even students, though students would join us, called like we were by something helpless, something that had sent up a flare, a distress call. We were free and needed a mission and a damp place to work things out, but could we ever sabotage our parents' dumb processes? Could we change the world? Could we scam money from the government? We always left drunk and beatific. You with me? Here we go on one of our travels, facing the wonky pub at the end of the small square, all black tarmac and closed shops, rain pelting down, advance scouts for some grand enterprise we were proud to be part of but about which we knew nothing. How we clung to one another. Didn't we? No. We each galloped forward as though alone. No. We stood, transfixed. No. A gull landed in the square and limped toward us; on its back, nestled across the strong brown wings, was a skinny white dog, a terrier.

Spirit Path

The bellringer — remember him? — marker of our time, doler out of a greenish afternoon, slate-grey sleet-chill morning, items of our valley allowance, temporally speaking, did I say he was blind? Anyway, he has decided (it has been formally decided) that his apprentice will take over his afternoon bells while a village woman — Song Wei! — will lead him every day down from his eyrie, down from his nest in the trees, down from his knoll near the North Gate, down the path to the frigid shrine where I write, so he can take his place beside me and make his painstaking characters.

He's writing his memoirs (no kidding). Here he is, bent over, his cheek so close to the page that I'm afraid he'll paint his terrible eyes, using a very fine brush to shape his story. (My body's in turmoil. Song's arm grazed mine when I helped her settle him at his table.) You have no inkling of his slowness. All the time he breathes into his gloved hands, little grunts of effort, and his tongue, ruddy and moist from a quick trip inside, points at me from the corner of his mouth.

With his chin in his hand, he looks like a boy, the boy he was. And is that a tear or a trick of the light? He's dreamy, in this poised state, like the heron — remember him? Perhaps this is the way he looks before releasing the timber to strike the bell. What is he reporting? Something deep and dark, no doubt, something of import to leave us when he dies.

"What are you writing?" I ask.

"The story of the bell."

"Ah. How can you write?"

He makes no sign of having heard. But he is writing. Perhaps light is all that can confuse us, and he cannot see light. He commits his brush strokes with confidence.

PENETRATING THE INTERIOR

Dark that won't brighten no matter what. No hills or mountains or sky. I remember being a boy with my mum and dad. I remember spending whole days with my wife and our son when we had a boy of our own. The two times get confused. Somebody threw somebody in the air and somebody gasped and somebody caught somebody. Hours at home preparing a script and going out to buy milk, then coming home to supper and a movie. Before bed someone was shouting. Blue-green anger surged under the busy engine, the family, until its parts flew apart, landing me here, bump skip bounce, arse over teakettle, fresh blood, ouch.

Clothes drying around the storehouse braziers. No electricity because the lines are down, no doubt knocked out by a fallen branch or tree.

My writing companion could not bear to abandon his bell, and he disliked being led by a woman, so Song Wei has been dismissed and it's my job to fetch him as soon as I hear the first afternoon bell. He works away beside me, while I sit in meditation.

It was almost night when I took him home to his hut. "Thank you," he said.

"What is it like to be blind?"

"Dark. What does the world look like now?"

"Dark."

"Are you going to the temple?"

"I have been asked to watch the children."

"A good thing to do!" He nodded and I made my way down the slippery path and through the temple yard and past the warm storehouse.

The children were making balls out of wet leaves and throwing them at one another. They ran along the shore of the swollen pond and wanted to be chased. Sparks from various fires streamed into the black sky. Geese burst into the valley and splashed down. The running and chasing churned a smell of rot from the earth. Then the children surged uphill and I followed: they were all splayed in the courtyard like flattened stars.

At night prayers there was a smell of drying laundry. My chest and neck hurt. I had a sharp pain in my leg and lower back. I was sore all over, but almost warm. An owl hooted. The kids would be asleep. Not a whisper of wind and nothing in the sky.

Spirit Gate

The bellringer and I have moved into the library on the coldest wettest days since our pen and brush won't make distinct shapes on soggy paper. The library braziers burn day and night, tended by two monks working in shifts. We all have aches now. Gall bladder and large intestine. Necks and shoulders. *Jiushu* monks will arrive next week. I fell asleep during Silken Movements. Dreamed of chopping down trees. I fell asleep when receiving a wood-and-metal release. Dreamed of that Norwegian hotel overlooking the three roads converging on the bridge where a river churned. Of course metal is the mother of water. Of course metal controls wood. Somewhere nearby is a drip, singular and significant in all the rain falling from heaven and from the tall bamboo.

Lesser Palace

More storms then a break in the rain and an evening of stories, accounts of the time before rocks and rivers.

Lesser Rushing

Who's down there calling in the long cloud on the river? A swan, I think, a swan not yet white, a young swan in the mist, calling. Sky's a dull dead screen. Not a young sky.

Our son, when my wife and I separated, changed into someone I didn't know, going to her place from mine and to my place from hers, no one to know what that was like but him. There were times at the door, his face pale, his eyes on mine for a moment before he leapt, wrapping his legs around my hips and burrowing there, young mammal, that provided all warmth to my marsupial heart. But what happened in that second it took to let him go?

Yang Fire

Water runs into wood. Smoke from braziers rises into stars burning above our heads. A fit of sneezing.

FRONT VALLEY

My blind brother waved his brush in the air. "What happened to the village woman, the one who used to bring me here?"

"Song Wei?" I said. "It's just as well you fired her. She's pregnant. Her eyes are too bright, even though she tries to hide them."

He crouched over his table and dipped his brush in ink. "She is beautiful?"

"Yes."

"As beautiful as the American actress?" His lips curved. "Last year her scent was everywhere."

"Imogen and Song Wei are both beautiful," I said.

"Song Wei, Imogen," he said. "You are naming people?"

"Why not? The master has given me a new master."

"I don't care. For me all women are clouds." He screwed his face up, pursing his lips and tilting his head, sour, mischievous. "In America I was called Frank."

The *jiushu* monks arrived, tall and silent, their robes redolent of burnt mugwort, to ignite their tiny conical towers at bladder points along our spines. They arranged us in rows on the storehouse mats, set their beacons alight, and patrolled among us.

Their seriousness was unnerving. But I felt warmer, with fewer aches, after my treatment.

Back Creek

"When struck," Frank said, "the bell balances the Great and the Going Away, water and fire. She balances the blood. She was forged in mountains a thousand miles from here, in the heart of a land of warring kingdoms. The furnace pit roared and glowed for three days and four nights, and at the moment the bell lost its fluid nature, a boy was born in the palace across the river to a wild prince and the local princess, and when the bell was hung in the monastery peace came to the region.

"The boy and his father and mother were untouched by loss for thirteen years, but then one day the monastery was overrun by bandits. Enraged at the sight of outlaws carrying off the temple's treasures, the boy drew his sword and rode in pursuit and at dawn came upon a wagon toppled into a river and the upturned bell full of bloody water."

Wrist Bone

Deep in the wild forest is said to be a large square pavilion of white stone inside a circle hedge of red berries. Inside the pavilion a circle of river stones, a square of reeds, a circle of clay figures, a square body of water contained by green marble sides, and in the centre of the pool a round island with four gates; in the middle of the island a small roofless pentagonal temple with a moat and a single entrance, south. Inside the temple a fountain. Water rushes from the temple fountain into the moat, through each gate back to the pool.

When you pass from our world through the gateless hedge into the white stone pavilion the squares and circles come so quickly one after the other that by the time you're standing in front of the temple you'd swear you had been travelling a long time, and when you step inside the temple, the fountain is so loud that you keep hearing voices, Someone calling your name over and over.

Yang Valley

We were both in our own dreams until Frank sneezed three times. He cleared his throat and spat. He touched my arm.

"So the prince organised the rebuilding of the temple and supervised the rehanging of the bell . . . those were terrible war years . . . and named himself Abbot and established a sect of monks who forged bells and smuggled them out at night into the divided world while the dead of endless skirmishes washed up at their gates. Within a few years thirty million families had been destroyed and yet many monasteries and temples had new bells."

He performed a flourish with his brush between his thumb and forefinger planted on the paper, then tilted his head back. "One night the bell did not sound, the palace was sacked, and the royal family cut to pieces, their limbs hung on the monastery gate. The old abbot escaped a valley filled with flames." Frank returned to his brush strokes.

"What happened to him?"

"He went out into the world. His monks were massacred around him in this valley, by our river. Oldest Grandfather was bearer of our bell."

The timbers of West Shrine are black and wet where they touch the earth. Some boards need replacing. But above our heads, his bent to his writing, cheek smudged with ink, mine angled to look up into the gloom, birds in the silver rafters rest from the rain.

West Shrine was built a long time ago to shelter conversations with God. We should be able to hear words in the thing built to house them. We should be able to see characters in the shape of these beams. The day after tomorrow I and my brother monks from Leopard Pass will board a bus to the next town and take a plane to the first city of our tour. Gone out, like the old abbot, into the world.

You are furious at me. What's wrong? (When I was young I'd frighten my sister by pretending to be dead, and once she was under my spell I'd spring back to life.) You want me invisible? You want me not to exist? You are always trying to see through me and I'm always ducking and weaving, a thin man, fast as glass, right?

After shouts and screams from the village, two men staggered bleeding into the storehouse. ("Who are these wild people?" the master wanted to know.) Two men with knife wounds, such small slits and so much blood, their eyes white, froth on both pairs of lips.

Nourish the Old

The two men lay side by side on the storehouse floor, their wounds dressed, faces and arms pale, while two monks ran their hands over their torsos and limbs, gathering and dispelling *qi* . . .

"All the men of my family become blind," Frank said. He touched my back with his forehead. "I was glad to see America."

Outside the storehouse, the sky was utterly white, with clouds massed on the horizon. Once I was a bird and loved this wide view that meant travel and held it in my heart for so long that it kicked me twice a year. The faster the wingbeat the swifter each flight between cloudbanks, surely ocean down there, surely some merchant container ship, and human again — can't stay bird long — human and up to something, I couldn't even take in the view without question.

The master bowed to me. Zhou Yiyuan waved an arm as he hurried on his way down the storehouse path from visiting his wounded men. Frank clutched my sleeve and would not let go. Snot fell from his nose. The sun came out and beautifully lit the villagers and monks as they hurried around the grounds attending to ordinary things after these days of rain. Red-and-black robes. Pink shirts. Purple head-cloths.

Branch to the True

A baby was crawling on the bridge toward the monastery as the three of us left. No mother or aunt to be seen. I scooped her up and she snuggled in my arms as the mother appeared from the forest at the end of the bridge.

All three of us were sick on the bus. Each of us held *hoku*, the valley between thumb and forefinger. How anyone, much less these thousands of people, can find their way through the maze of an airport and complete all the security rituals and ticket inspections in time to board the plane is now beyond me. I felt like a young bull, a sweet-eyed calf who had lost his mother and was destined for veal. If I wasn't already steeped in shame I'd begin to moan.

Once our plane rose above the clouds bright sunshine illuminated stately slabs of white mist, baroque, rococo, magnified beyond mobility, too slow for our eyes, dense as marble, eternal, until we landed at the large airport at *Z*.

In the racket of television, refrigerated food-and-drink machines, hidden fans stirred the air, and the human voice could hardly be heard. The cover of *National Geographic* showed the picture of a child with chimp mouth and flyaway hair.

Found Earliest Child. 3.3-million-year-old bones discovered.

An owlish three-year-old girl from Ethiopia. What kind of innocence was this? I tapped Silk Bamboo Hollow, the end of the eyebrow, to clear the damp. Could the world be more precarious or more surprising?

We sat on moulded plastic chairs, taking turns visiting the airport bathroom until our next flight was announced.

An oval window on the small plane looked out at the silver nose of the propeller. Soon the blades vanished. A kind of vertigo. The plane so small that all the passengers had window seats. Blake's "dark valley" was behind us; ahead were three jewelled cities. *Manipura*. The novelist Ōe quotes Blake. As does Tagore. I'm recording fevered thoughts. The lost child, the found child, the ancient child. The poison tree, the knowledge tree. The Plutonium, dark throat of the earth, where Ulysses was said to have descended. A Sybil on a knoll shuddering in ecstasy. The cloud Lord speaking to the Lord of Destiny about football. The building of the Manchester Ship Canal. The Iron Worker's Memorial Bridge. My wife's warm arms, some last time. Spiralling down. Where would we land? When would all this be destroyed? When would the big bits be retrieved from chaos and assembled for a new winter coat, no one the wiser? We were travelling back in time. Wisdom *was* a fool's game. Loud and bumpy and unsophisticated.

SMALL SEA

The village airport was a dark field and the village itself a cluster of lights on a hillside beside miles of factories and worker housing. We were met by the two famous exiles who drove us through interconnected courtyards and narrow lanes and covered passages to an old wood house. The central fire-pit had been tiled and we sat on cushions. The prophet spoke of the simple life they led now. Her husband said, yes, they were happy. She told us he walked miles every day, even through this snow and bitter cold, while she tracked down world leaders on the Internet. They fed us vegetables they had grown in the shadow of the great factories. He had his students; she kept up correspondence with the outer world. They were still afraid of arrest and deportation, though nothing had happened for years.

"Time is required for the dust to settle," he said.

"He is too patient," she said.

"Time is part of the original agreement," he said. "Human time does not count."

They both smiled.

After our meal, we sat and drank tea. The woman asked me why I became an actor.

"I have no idea."

My brother monks gazed about, as if to catch some important detail: drips on the icy bare branches outside the window; a spear hung on the wall across from a triptych of Mongolian warriors; a parrot on a branch beside the prophet's stool.

Her husband said, "The temperature is rising and soon it will snow again and snow deep."

The woman fed the parrot a chunk of fruit. Her husband watched her. A monk arrived to lead us to the evening meeting with traditional doctors.

"I am not patient," she said. "I have some waves to make."

He said, "I have a sister teaching in Paris. I hope one day to teach in Paris."

TRUE SHOULDER

The monastery overlooked a river and the site of an old battle-ground. The land descended to the river in terraces developed long ago, now smooth white snowfields, and in the vague distance a long rail bridge spanned the river. We performed in a small tapestried room. The doctors watched us demonstrate access routes to the Great Point.

"You are like old warriors," one said. "Five elements has not been taught for years. Your armour must be tarnished and rusty. The points are just points."

We gathered in a large hall. On the other side of glass doors snow fell heavily, the flakes slow and aimless, into a courtyard. Tables were set up and monks chosen to receive treatments. I was stiff. I could barely move my arms and fingers. I couldn't free my clogged joints and clenched muscles as I hunted points on an old man with extreme pain in his neck and shoulders and in his hips and thighs.

Taking his pulses I saw a tumbleweed trapped against a prairie fence and a magpie fluttering briefly in a dawn sky, a car passing, children's faces pressed to the windows, thin snow whirling by the rear tires. I knew I was one of the children, but where was the old man? Something was pushing him, pushing him forward; he wanted to go; he did not want to be pushed.

The monks we worked on were all in pain. We explained that pain was a bridge from one place to another. We encouraged each monk, as his points were held, to see the places pain bridged. The old man I'd treated turned to a doctor taking rapid notes. He tapped the doctor's knee. "Pain," he said, "is the bridge between me and death."

The doctor returned to his notes. The old man leaned toward me and laughed. In a voice so quiet on one else heard it, he said, "I may choose not to go there yet."

On TV screens back at the big airport young people danced around an elderly man in a tuxedo who held a long microphone like a magic wand. Each tried to outdo the others in wild leering wide-eyed leaps at the camera, giving exaggerated thumbs-up signs every few minutes. The old standards of rank have clearly broken down.

Sigmund Freud died at the outset of the Second World War. He managed last words: "Dog people run things when Babel falls."

And Dedaelus invented images, Pasiphae's bull, the labyrinth, and wings to fly him safe and sound to the sun and home.

Poor Icarus. We are such a busy species. Tumbleweed alongside the creaky warrior. Brittleness and the urge for self-sacrifice. How do we keep pliant and receptive in this image-strewn and deceptive maze where genetic research will save our souls? Here we go. The dreamy long view, melting linkages. Stop struggling! For sure we don't know who we are. Bones are intact longer than flesh. The three-year-old Ethiopian girl entered the long wind of history and the wind changed direction and her fossils rattled free. Yes, she was a girl who suckled her mother's breast. Yes, she saw the world with unique eyes. But she is nobody's ancestor.

I'm trying to tell the truth. I'm never fair to you. I know we're bound together in some way I don't understand. Your life continues, somewhere, perhaps without indecision. Perhaps it's summer where you are. These are ways of getting our feet on the ground. Freud's death. The little girl's death, before Ethiopia. Artificial wings. Ambiguity. Fledged truth. Can I bring us both safely home to River Mountain?

Upper Arm Shu

A memorable lunch of noodles in broth, spices difficult to identify. A cheerful monk I met some years ago sat across the table. Astonishingly, he took from his pocket a publicity photograph of Imogen and passed it to me. It was a still from one of her recent films. She is shown side-on, emphasising the adolescent shape of her flanks and hips, looking down at the ground, and seems to be standing in a deluge of rain, her face glistening with droplets.

An evening demonstration for a handful of doctors, one of whom had a bag full of old texts, medical and spiritual, from which he consulted diagrams and anatomies throughout our sessions. I was flustered and blundered in a daze through the long discussion that followed.

Sky Gathering

Past midnight, giddy from lack of sleep, we asked where these people had come from.

"They are patients from the mental hospital," a doctor said.

Another doctor opened an old book and said: "Have the energy levels in the Great Points been measured and compared?"

We couldn't stop laughing. The doctors had been drinking and were loud. One played old songs on the violin. My head sank for a moment. I heard voices from outside. "Where are my brothers?"

"They are in the parking lot building a snowmonk."

GRASPING THE WIND

Another flight after a short sleep. The future seems to be coming from the past. Snow on the fields and the trees jagged with frost.

When seeking points on a young woman I found myself imagining a whole life with her. What work we might do together, where we'd travel, how we'd educate our children.

Later, walking with a doctor from Saskatoon, talking about healing and the delights of combining allopathic treatments with five-element approaches, I looked up and saw a house burning. Snow blowing down the street hit our faces and blurred my vision and I had to blink and turn away. Ice crystals sparkled on the reeds by the wide river. The house stood in a row of other identical houses and was brilliantly lit but not on fire.

For a moment the young woman of the morning lived with me in that house. That was where we raised our kids.

CROOKED WALL

Today I worked on a patient who wore a band of fat around her waist in which was stored a million years of abuse. She had developed an impressive list of symptoms. The bones of her spine were fused and walking was difficult. Doctors had diagnosed diseases. She had accepted each diagnosis. I palpated her gall bladder meridian, then focused on two points: one for the little girl free of illness, one for her ancestral line. Afterward the physicians in the room remarked on the youth of her face. Although she was not free of pain, she felt peaceful and, for the first time in a long while, hopeful.

Through the airport windows we watched men and women steer machines round the banked snow, lights blinking in the blowing orange flakes. Then the machines dashed for the buildings and people in fat jumpsuits and puffy headgear leapt out and disappeared underground. A plane was sprayed with antifreeze. Daylight filled the runways with grey and white streaks.

As our plane took off my bits and pieces felt nearly integrated. The temperature plunged and wind worried up what snow the horizon grasses could no longer anchor; the war-toll rose; human population increased; icecaps north and south melted. What drove me down and threatened to bury me in the past — compost, deadfall — had been shifted by an upsurge. Wings were still attached. The wax had not melted. The visible sun and the echo under mountains were tapping each of my toes as I held my breath. Rivers meander until the slow sea calls them down. Oxygen circles with blood. And she will come and I will talk to her about *River Mountain Bell*, a new play in which she is my wife and I am the abbot-prince.

On our way home we found sunshine once again above the clouds and were confident our trip had been a success and that some reversal had occurred, was occurring.

We trudged behind the luggage cart toward the terminal. Behind the tall windows were businessmen and women with digital devices organising their realms.

I must apologise to you. I must apologise. I do not know what you do. I do not know what you do in your own unassuming work. I am no doubt proceeding as you expected. But I had high hopes.

A young woman in the airport loading area, as we waited for the bus, received a phonecall and howled. It sounded at first like laughter. She turned to us and said, "He's already dead," then looked at the sky, tears rolling from her eyes. A squat grey-haired woman ran out of the airport doors, arms spread wide, and the young woman warded her off.

I must apologise. This isn't what I set out to do. Confusions. Interruptions. Problems of foreground and background. Soon we will be home. I will try, in the coming days, to see how it went wrong; it is crucial, especially now, that you have a life of your own.

Until now my task has been to record each day's thoughts, to get them down fresh, before they fall to any depth in memory and are impossible to retrieve without being distorted by the upheaval. The trouble is there is an active warp; the fault-line that divides imagination from memory is unstable. But I wanted to write the physical world and arrive at an untold story, and I have failed. I wanted story as schist, irregular truth, but any notation will bear the pattern of the warp.

MIDDLE SHOULDER SHU

I went one last time to my father's rest home.

"Why are you always so sad?" he asked me.

"I'm not," I said.

"When will you let it all go?"

"I'm happy, Dad. I doubt myself, of course. But I'm not miserable."

"You have always worried, just like your mother. As if any kind of belief would be a mistake. It's fear of losing things makes you worry. When will you give it up?"

"Dad. Everything is okay."

"Well, I won't last the year. And your mother's crazy. Perhaps we are finished here."

It was very cold and the valley was full of snow and wind, snow blowing off the branches, and crows wheeling like bits of dark come loose from night and the bamboo bent under heavy crystals impossible to ignore.

SKY WINDOW

My life has been a steady journey here. Born in England, beginning of the war, I fought Germans and Japanese in schoolyard battles through the early fifties, and on weekends dreamed up elaborate conflicts where I was a solitary soldier in enemy territory, scaling hillsides, crouched behind rock outcrops, checking the sky and horizon for signs, men rising up before me, dark-coated and massive, wanting only to rend and devour, and telling myself one truth: they are like me, simple, unstoppable, hurt, visible, and knowable, while more waited, half-glimpsed in a night forest, full of cunning and bloodlust — other, elsewhere, not quite of this world — while I tried many escapes, sailed to New York with my parents, flew to Vancouver, back to a life at RADA, then London's theatre hub, spokes to a host of plays and film shoots. You. You. You. Here.

December

Sky Hood

IT TAKES AN HOUR FOR TWO BLACK HOLES to coalesce, and when they blend they groan, they sing, but light's different, light from stars travels in waves, particles, silence. The shivering beggar under the bridge deck chants as he displays his broken weapons; children at his side dance like monkeys. It is a dark time of year to go home. There's the bell. *The bell is haunted.* So the black hole and the black hole meet for an hour (their hotel has seen better days), and for an hour all heads incline, buildings lean, tides twitch, and then they return to their lives.

Do you know the human gesture to protect us from life's unmentionables? I don't mean the head bowed in surrender; I don't mean the reactive leap backward or the sucker-punch. Even as a child I saw the end of such goofy dramatics. Houses are built room by room, you learn the pattern, and in England as I watched my father brick up the back door and cut another facing south, I knew my fingers didn't want to know the ins and outs of renovation based on someone else's plan (Mum again). It seemed and still seems fickle, naively hopeful work. No, I'm talking about a personal gesture, subtle-like for the camera, almost a tic, but universal, too. What you are doing now while your eyes sweep over the gaps between the words looking for someone — she might wander from copse to lane and you might miss the moment — still carries me. There must be a gesture to let in what's needed.

Cheek Bone Crevice

It was late when we crossed the bridge home. The master welcomed us in his hut and asked each of us to speak. After we'd finished, silence, and then he said, "A poet nun from North Valley will sing for us tomorrow evening."

Later I was walking the paths, looking for evidence of my nests and finding none, when Song Wei appeared through the trees. We bowed in the old way and she asked what I was looking for.

"Birds," I told her. "I'm looking for lost birds. So many species have vanished from the valley."

She stood watching me while every branch dripped and snow creaked under her feet. Was she beautiful? Oh, yes.

Palace of Hearing

My favourite pen is missing and I borrowed a brush from Frank. The snow has almost gone. When things are lost I despair of setting my feet on the ground. The madman is among us again, inside our grounds, screaming and laughing. Last night the bell rang after one outburst, then rang a second time, even though the timber had been double-tied and the knot was still secure this morning.

O

Bright Eyes   Yang Water

All the nests are lost and the round stones set inside are scattered.
Sometimes I wake in the morning straight into anguish about
money, then realise it's not money now but something else that's
scarce. And not hope or joy, but a subtle version of being here.
I fashioned the nests too quickly and didn't know what I was
doing. The poet sang last night.

Gathered Bamboo

About snow and war and exile. Her voice thin as a child's. And
then the stage was empty again. Perhaps poetry is a way to
empty things.

My parents met at a dance hall called the Tin Bin during
the war, a time young couples met at dances on Saturday nights.
My father loved my mother steadily for seventy years, while her
love for him, small at the outset, grew to a late crescendo. This
is the simple version, the family version. I was born; my sister
was born.

When the number of players on the stage is exactly right, the
audience relaxes. There is fullness. In the following silence, the
distant murmur of a winter stream is all that's needed.

Eyebrow Flush

The hill terraces are silver green, made flat by men for grain:
there lentils, there rice; the valley bottom is flooding, snow
at the margins, standing water black in the middle. The bell,

certainly haunted, calls out, and echoes from the edge of the valley sound like a jazz trio — Bobo Stenson, Anders Jorman, Paul Motian — as they carry the vibration of the mother metal. Frank keeps to his hut and North Gate Shrine.

Paths ascend from the valley north and south, but we do not use the south paths across the river. There have been terrible battles up and down those slopes. This is where Song's rapists came from, and ghosts of thin warriors still drift like smoke among the trees. The north paths are beloved, well-travelled: we send monks with questions climbing the mountain, and from the mountain come answers.

In a New World dream my father is driving east into the Rockies; behind him on the coast Mother's burning through the second season of her show; they have had a ferocious battle about us kids. At the next motel, Dad turns on the TV and hears poems sung in a language he doesn't understand, though he does understand such heartbreak. At the bathroom mirror he can't cut through the whiskers on his cheeks, on his chin, even though the blade is new. His knuckles are sunburnt from the drive and he is lonely. Again and again he pulls the razor over his face, remembers England, each job, each child. The motel is like a private ward, despite the poems, and sleep's a sudden blanket. He dreams of his son playacting, his daughter full of petulant secrecy as his wife, in her TV series, *Three Becomes Four*, gives birth to a new baby girl.

The master sat in his winter robes across the small table in a corner of the storehouse library. We had the brazier for company, a stack of wood and the large north-facing window. Afternoon light energised the pattern on his wide sleeve — swirls of green and yellow — when his arm rose.

"Why are you still here?" he said.

We listened to the rushing stream outside.

He looked over his shoulder, then down at his hands. "D'you think this valley needs outsiders?"

Together we watched his rough thin restless hands chase each other.

He smiled. "Once the bell was a stranger. I was pleased with your report."

Sun shone into the library. Webs high in the corners trembled.

"When I was a boy I owned a fox," he said. "I kept him in a wood cage and we travelled round the countryside. We were a single being. When we came to a town I set him free and we walked up and down the streets."

My throat, the muscles, thickened, and heat throbbed behind my eyes. "I belong here," I said.

"No," he said. "But there is a wildness in you that does." He waved his hand. "You are unaware of this."

I have the rest of the afternoon in the library to myself. Since he left, a woodpecker has been drumming from the grove of trees behind the storehouse. I write at the low table, listening to the fire's crackling wood, while a flock of crows is busy in the trees. I am calm. Things can be forgotten. Purposely left behind. I no longer have the sense of impending disaster I have construed in myself variously as anxiety, worry, suspicion, doubt, self-criticism, paranoia.

Imogen's like a carefully wrapped orphan left in a basket on a river, back of winter. The current tugs at the basket as buds on the willows begin to swell.

CROOKED CURVE

The day was cold and my hands numb, so I was hurrying along the path, on my way to a session with one of the settlement women, when I saw them. Mist lay across the river, dark on top and silver underneath, night already pushing in from the east so the trestle supports were invisible and the bridge deck seemed to float. An insubstantial world, then, with a stage.

The man in a long grey coat was hunched over lighting a cigarette, intent on his cupped hands, and a boy, no doubt his son, was engaged in his own small stooping play. They seemed together yet entirely separate — loose from their tribe — on the platform in the mist. The man's hand wavered a moment above his son's head. This was it, you see, the gesture: a kind of roof, as simple as that.

The settlement woman had been suffering from a month-long headache. Her husband had recently fallen and could not work, her grown son was returned from a failed endeavour in the port, and her younger children were hungry. Fire point in gall bladder. Water point in liver. Gall Bladder-38 *Yangfu*. Liver-8 *Ququan*.

Fifth Place

Up from the pupil of the eye, halfway to the crown of the head. A point through which the bladder looks up at the sky. Clouds like a ploughed grey field. Hold with right middle finger.

Second point *Mingmen*, Gate of Life, ministerial fire, on the spine just below the second lumbar vertebra. Hold with the left middle finger.

Zhou Yiyuan stood at the door.

"Nothing for a farmer to do," he said. "It's all done. A cup of wine. A cup of thick wine. Nothing else to plant, nothing to harvest. A cup of thick wine."

Drop left finger down to *Du-3 Yaoyangguan*. Lumbar Yang Gate. To dispel wind-damp.

RECEIVING LIGHT

The high slopes pure white. The sun-filled room cold without fire. What was lost came home in another form (a lost girl, love between father and son, a point, the master's fox, my pen) as I worked on her migraine. The session cut short because her baby was screaming. As she nursed I stood behind her and held Yang White, both sides, and looked down at the swirls of black hair on the infant's head. She told me when I enquired that Song Wei was ill.

Babies are difficult to dislodge. I listened to ice in the river, then to the nearby knocking of men strengthening or repairing roofs. Momentary wind through the trees outside.

HEAVENLY CONNECTION

It snowed in the night and my past seemed far away, just a white shimmer out there in the bamboo. One of the babies cried at dawn amid the murmur of prayer; then the bell rang. Snow has flattened every blade of grass yet the young bamboo springs back if given a vigorous shake. I met a village couple on the temple path, an infant tied to the woman's belly, the man carrying a bundle of sticks. Tonight it's bright in the library. I am grass. How is Song Wei?

REFUSING CONNECTION

Toward the end of the short day, a monk was etching the margin of the bamboo forest, carefully picking his way through the white drifts at the shore of a long frozen puddle, dragging the old bamboo rake. He paused, then turned to look behind him.

Zhou Yiyuan lurched to catch up and as they met, both swayed, off balance, each leaning away from the other—

A moment of great stress. Enough of routines, practices, observances and rituals, a new pattern is emerging! The healing line, true for seven hundred years, is faltering. Wood. Water. Wood. Water creates wood. Water is the daughter of metal, grandmother of fire.

Zhou Yiyuan pushed the monk into the bamboo, then turned in slow motion and strode uphill through fat drifts.

Once upon a time when I was a boy I ran naked down a road in the middle of a summer night to a rough beach, tide high and black, choppy waves rolling in every direction, and leapt from an outcrop into the sea.

JADE PILLOW

My only non-actor friend in Vancouver was a forensic social worker whose job was to ascertain mental competency and make psychiatric recommendations for men who had committed violent crimes. The day before Jake drove me to the airport, on my way here, one of his clients had lifted a hammer from a shelf in a hardware store and bludgeoned four shoppers, so Jake was distracted. "The big figures of madness," he said, "the Caesars, Christs, Hitlers never surface any more, what with the availability and the power of the new drugs!"

Something is broken. Something is leaking, this world into that, that into this. I don't know. Do you? Tree branches now cracked will soon be torn away. New buds shrivel on the fallen branches. Time freezes the apples left for winter birds. Space is altered since I saw what I saw. The valley is filling with snow. The bell is haunted. The man screams in the night, though it's hard to tell whether it's a man or a child or a lost animal. Perhaps it is a baby crying. I dreamed of another baby girl, this one safely tied in a tree by her mother, using her own coarse black hair, wrapped against the cold and out of the reach of dangerous men, yet terrified and alone.

Morning has been quiet, but now there's wind on the river striating the mercuric surface, rushing through the lake fields, and birds wheel in the next teeming storm.

Celestial Pillar

The baby trussed up in the tree will not leave me alone. Now she sucks her thumb and watches massive white clouds with black bellies roll in from the southwest above the portion of the road and river she can see from her branch. Her mother must have forgotten her by now.

There's news of military activity on the southern plains; there are rumours of government spies in the region. Snow has buried the pile of refuse that clings to the village site, which a year ago was meadow verging rice paddy.

I was walking the snow-path at the edge of the settlement, trying to think what the master might want (he has told me we will speak tomorrow), when I met Zhou Yiyuan.

"Is your sister well?" I asked.

"You are not used to fighting," he said, his breath pluming.

"I saw what happened to her," I said. "What could I have done?"

"Interfered," he said.

"I heard she was sick. Is she all right?"

We stood in snow-filled hills, hammered by cold wind. I had the sense I was very small and must make the most of every moment, no matter what the content. The valley seemed infected with crime.

Great Shuttle

Chainsaws work the fallen trees. They've been running for days now, little gas engines needling the air, sectioning the old pines felled by wind and heavy snow.

"These strangers are wild people," the master said. "I wonder if they wish to remain wild." He sat near the fire. The bell sounded, muffled by the falling snow. But for the tinkling coals and his raspy breath, we had been in silence for a long time. He cocked his head, listening. "It is as though our bones are singing." His head fell, his chin resting on his chest. Then he twitched, and his head rose again. "You are going to tell me," he said in a low voice. "You are going to tell me what has happened. Wait." He looked straight ahead, his eyes half-closed, a frail smile on his lips, and when he spoke again, his voice was brittle. "What is that?" He pointed into the shadows.

My pen lying against the wall.

I retrieved it and wiped off the dust.

"I have received a letter from the actress," he said. "I would like you to respond. Where is it? Wait." He leaned forward. "Tell me the point in River Mountain that will heal what has been broken. No. First tell me what you have done."

Shame burned like frost on my skin. I clutched my pen but wasn't able to say anything.

This afternoon the ink flows too quickly. Each word threatens to become a small pond, the nib skating lightly, isolate letters inflating themselves. It is as though I am not where I am. Just now, while walking in the woods at the correct moment doing the precise chore the way I've been taught, my head filled with light and my eyes wouldn't focus and the world tilted. It feels as though I've been telling lies, doing something I have no right to do. I'm someone I have no right to be.

A monk brought the letter to me in the library a moment ago. Imogen has read an Internet blog about the one-point technique and says we must guard our secrets so they do not spill into the social media. Ironic, really, because she has been a factor in our exposure; her fame has already drawn attention to us. She wants to know if she will still find our order intact when she returns next year. Do we need money? I am to write to her in the master's name, saying yes to the money, and reassuring her that she will find all she seeks in our valley.

Wind Gate

The biggest storm yet kept us awake all night. In the dark an army of demons screamed and tore at the buildings. The bell rang of its own accord. Trees crashed at the edge of the frozen fields, and this morning four of the oldest pines were lying, roots in the air, obliterating the unused East Gate. No power. Still dim at midday, with cold air from the north and its smell of snow.

I must think how to phrase my response to Imogen's letter, to settle her mind about the monastery and its destiny, to say we are calm, unaffected by chaos. Calm? In fact, we are all freezing to death. I hope to God it's warm where you are. The problem is always how to trace a path from one unknown toward another, how shade the closing distance, and do it all without hesitation. Even when subject and object are in place and all that remains to be found is the verb, I'm in a cold sweat. I can't stop shivering and my knees lock and I can't find my feet. I feel as though I'm translating every word from my father's dead language that I only heard when I was too young to understand it.

Tomorrow will you walk with me along the river and help me find the valley point to balance all discrepancies? If you do, I'll write the letter.

LUNG SHU

We had a winter meeting, monks and villagers, and several elders spoke. I had something to say, but when I tried I could not utter a word. Back in my stage days it was necessary when facing a large crowd to lose focus, just for a second, in order to find my lines and the audience in the same room. Now when I lose focus all I feel is danger. The acting world is not the world of contemplation. The last time I stood in front of a panel of doctors it did not go well. The air thronged with questions, all unasked, all mine.

Old women spoke at the meeting, almost singing, like children before they need the world, garbling words due to lack of teeth and the intense cold. Short leathery old sages with round lined faces. The cold grey air hung in thin light from the storehouse windows; toward the rafters smoke gathered in a brown pall. An old woman danced foot to foot, crazy as a pot, and yet the music in her voice turned every face in her direction.

The old monks nodded their heads and she really began to wail, her hands flying about her ears.

JUEYIN SHU

I crossed the bridge, walked the river west. (Do you feel anything? Nothing? A sick feeling? Here we fucking go again?) Song Wei's skin, flashlights, the boys and men. (Is it here where the reeds along the curved bank are blood red in winter?) Probably upstream was the wrong direction. Back at the bridge ice sheets were shattering against the pilings.

Zhou Yiyuan joined me and we teetered on crusted snow slowly east toward the gorge, dainty steps. After about ten minutes huge flakes began to fall. "We have something to unravel together," he said.

"What?" I asked.

"You know," he said.

"No, I don't."

"Oh yes." He pranced like a madman, black hair swinging, upturned face all angles and disgust. He pushed me hard and I almost toppled into the purling water.

I regained my feet and looked down. Beneath his wet black hair his forehead was pale and vulnerable. "Do you want me to see your sister?"

Heart Shu

The memory of someone's death is enough; the day need not include anything else. The day of your death is already filled with itself. Weather heavy. Landscape muffled. Figures distant.

Governor Shu

I'm imagining what it will be like. Let me see if I have your death right. That winter after the friends visit. Brandy and milk in the microwave oven. Stain in the clawfoot tub. Your wildcraft remedy. The big house where you keep your things. I only want what might slip through your fingers when you cross that line. A clue, I think, that would serve me now.

I ran into the freezing dawn and found an intact nest!

Diaphragm Shu

So I visited Zhou Yiyuan and his sister. We sat on old carpets over the dirt floor beside a pile of dried mud and they showed me a small tree they had decorated with cloth stars, in my honour, for Christmas, for crissakes. I chanted with Zhou and his sister and some villagers round the fire in their room and in the dim light I could not tell if she was really pregnant. She seemed thin, her face gaunt.

Whisky flowed the winter of my wife's death. In Vancouver, I sat with best friends in front of their natural-gas fire while they held a throwaway lighter to their mortgage and, slightly nervous as they glanced at me, laughed about their success and my redundant divorce.

These villagers own next to nothing. More crowded in, smiling to see the tree. Zhou retreated to the shadows, anger threatening to erupt. Shivering children gathered outside the shack and stared in at us, their eyes quick and hungry, as we sipped tea, clutching our bowls. Then I walked uphill through the smoke from village fires and turned to look at the river, black gulf in the snowscape, and saw my own breath rising into night.

LIVER SHU

I fell into one of the seasonal streams that run this time of year down the north-facing hillside below an old battle site. Drawn again, you notice, to the wicked south paths, to the bend in the river where the rape took place. It was dark, early morning, and I wasn't properly awake, but stood in the reeds and stared a long time at the log Song Wei had been draped over, black bile in my throat, and then turned and slipped. I was no sooner in the shallow icy water than I was out, cursing the stars, recrossing the bridge to change my robe before climbing the hill to calm myself at the storehouse fire, and then trudging to the temple where I was late and bruised for silken movements.

GALL BLADDER SHU

The rest of the day was so: emotional hesitancy; look no one in the eye; curse myself and winter; do nothing but stare through the storehouse windows. I know why I fell. The valley point has to do with family and home and sex, and in that wheeling constellation I got lost. Must I have a plainer statement for you or for the master? What would you have me do? (Quit your whining, do I hear?)

Outside, the sky puffs up grey around the tall bamboo. Ice discs lie on the snow, one for each barrel under the storehouse roof; a small wave from a drop radiates to the barrel lip. Close my eyes, all I see is Imogen's body: once when I worked on her I fell into the plane of her belly between navel and pubic bone, at *Ren*-4, Gate of Origin, yin fire, the fire closest to heart's minister . . .

SPLEEN SHU

Here's mine. Family at the end of the universe, we sat together on the bed of our East Van house and watched *Star Wars*: laugh-track robots and idiot humans, incomparable adventure, pure noise and bombast. One becomes Four; Two becomes Five; Three becomes Six. What would they think of next? The father saves the son. The son saves the father. The son burns the father. In Vancouver before we separated we were a family of three at the end of the short December day, solstice tree in the corner hung with white lights. Popcorn passed from lap to lap. *Once upon a time.* Mandarin oranges peeled and divided. Tu Fu's translated poems on the floor. Meanwhile, in Ch'eng-tu, beyond the Ch'in Ling Mountains, Tu Fu found his thatch hut. The year 766 — Western count — Tibet about to invade again.

What are we concocting? Homunculus from a retort or binary
Yoda? *Remember it always, I will.* My father's ashes drifting off
Striding Edge in the Lake District. Now that valley. Now this
valley. Now the bell. Now my son. Now yours?

STOMACH SHU

It's Christmas Eve. I see my life stretched behind me, each
summer a vector, a blade, path to a place not home but like home:
a facsimile of home, and ahead there's Imogen in river light, in a
white dress, hair a curtain, a tall white swan with folded wings
stopped on the edge of the bridge. Somewhere, even now, you
breathe air. You go to sleep. Make a call. Mark your place in
the book before putting it down. Perhaps. Although I'm closer I
still can't find words to tell that I witnessed a brutal act and did
nothing. Can the place of rape be the valley point? The tether
between human and nature? Unimaginable, another person's
life. Mine included. Fathoms deep.

SANJIAO SHU

It's good to be alive, close to the bamboo and river, in the warm
storehouse library, studying this formal life represented in wood-
block prints. Black ink, white page. Stillness dozing inside paper.
The new shoots. The old. The new shoots the old. *Once Upon
a Time in the West.* The old West is the new East. Elsewhere
Christ's birth.

KIDNEY SHU

A thousand birds come down to the river, to the streams and
frozen ditches; flocks sing in the forest, gulls mutter on top

of the storehouse roof and a songbird calls from the warrior tree; bird tracks maze every white expanse. Imagine taking scissors and cutting the grey clouds to make a roof — and it isn't guesswork, clockwork or binary work, but a strict emphatic statement. A swift act to do with time, the absence of space. A pulse. Outgrowth of the human pulse. This feather as physical song. Invisible embrace in place of buildings.

SEA OF QI SHU

Eating the first meal today I broke a tooth. Wind and subzero temperatures, the exposed fallen grasses white and the bamboo whistling. Terrible, the end of teeth. When teeth start rotting and crumbling there's not much time left and every look from every person, if annoying, is a wondrous event. The achy path leads downhill, bump bump bump, rocks jagged and the climate wetter and colder, till I'm toothless, beyond pain, on a frosty skerry beach, my fingers numb, my lungs flapping like dead leaves.

LARGE INTESTINE SHU

All morning I collected fallen branches and broke them into pieces to burn, even the smallest twig, so the snow was free of leaves and bits of wood. From down here I watched Frank's distant figure strike the bell and slowly make his way back to his hut. Today's the finest, sunniest, coldest we've had in weeks. My tooth pain is gone. Villagers and monks came out to greet one another and stood blinking together, the men in ceremonial clothes and the women and children dancing from noon till now, till it's quiet. The blinding sun skips along the south hills, the pines bristling copper, and the combined smoke from our fires slinks east and the Northern Dipper, origin of yin and yang, faces half a moon and a sheer universe.

Gate of Origin Shu

Life has shape, shape and form, schedule. The rape point is blue, spiralling with energy. If I name it I implicate myself. Family is open to what will sprout. Other shapes, including who I was in the past, who you are, randomly drawn, unfinished, are the work of an amateur. What we do alone is useless. What we do alone is without form.

Small Intestine Shu

But answers seem less relevant than fresh snow on the mountain. Our roof is a long cloud blowing off the peak. This morning the bell rang and the monks chanted and the deficiencies and excesses arm-wrestled and the tea was cold and what did I care whether Frank greeted me or not? These healing places are warrens of disintegrating efficiency with too many patients, too few nurses, with diseases more and more specific and the hunt for causes ridiculous. This drug will target the toothless poet raving in the distance, five fields away. *That trial.* I am pregnant because I raped myself. *That syndrome.*

Bladder Shu

Bottom of the Shu ladder, just beginning the buttock hill climb. Fucking bell. Fucking monks. Fucking valley and river. Fucking tree. Fucking bamboo. What I wouldn't give for a coffee. Fucking snow.

JANUARY

MID-SPINE SHU

TODAY THE SAME AS YESTERDAY, WITH FREEZING RAIN, now a small storm passing over, with small winds. Except I'm in love and we are at war. A monk I don't know well said he thought our life here was complete, but that he wanted something more. A disturbing thing to say, and shocking that he should speak at all. There are four factions involved in border disputes and government forces are on the move. Mist veils the other side of the valley. The trees are like ghost armies. One moment there, the next gone. The sleet crackles with expectancy. We're chanting because penguins and polar bears have abandoned their centuries-old tracks and extinction is contagious and the edges of Wall Street are crumbling and billionaires can't help rolling on. A dead soldier in blue-and-white winter uniform rides the river ice. We pray for balance. The valley is apprehensive: rogue winds, some warm, some cold, run above the wild streams. It's hard to concentrate. My broken tooth does not hurt, but its jagged edge has torn my cheek. We chant the things lost or given up. We do not wait for anything. Even on a day like this, sodden and without colour, birds fly sideways down to the bridge timbers, perch, then fly off and out of sight, and children run along the paths and go quiet near shrines and the temple.

White Essence, Jade Ring Shu

Jewels on every branch when the rain briefly stops. We pray for long ceasefires. Let this be the end of wars, not the end of the world. Don't let all we love pass away. The fourth movement, *sehr langsam*, of Mahler's Fifth. Why did earth move from its place in the centre of the square formed by water, fire, metal and wood, to its present location between fire and metal? Did it happen when we understood that the centre was empty? That God was fishing another pond? The five-element diagram that looked like two integrated sand timers now resembles a star trapped in a house. The jig is up! We have been cosy and bored. As a father I wanted everything the mother had. Everything except pain and occupation. Water in my mouth tingles and shimmers. The broken tooth calls less often to the tongue. All over the valley the sound of water.

Upper Crevice

I've never worked so hard in my life. Service, I suppose. Not work. This moment, between sweeping the shrines and silken movements, is borrowed from a day of physical praise. Sun on the water. Amazing light through the clouds, and a boat, a boat pushing upstream, against the flow. Water, wind, reeds and chanting going east, while this boat steams west. Deep clouds, sun in shifting patches on distant snowy fields. Somewhere in these images is Einstein behind a desk, writing equations with his legs crossed. I'm tired and it's beginning to rain. Service is what we have called work, service to state, nation or God. A duty, a birthright, a horror of laziness? I don't have a name for work now.

Smoke puffs from the little crooked stack, and the boat rocks gently, grey weathered hull and plywood housing rattling with the chug of the motor, propeller surging the full river, ice on the margins, wind vexing prayer flags.

Second Crevice

The boat struggling upstream carried a father and three daughters, the middle sister beautiful, the family escaping skirmishes in the East province, the mother killed. With just a little fuel left, they had to come ashore. We fed them in the shabby camp below the monastery, didn't want them in the grounds, and Frank came down from his perch to bring them sufficient fuel to continue.

When they cast off I watched the father ease forward the throttle. The girls huddled in the lee of the wheelhouse and looked around at the flooding river, our buildings on the hillside, the mountain masked in thunderheads. Wrapped in their layers of clothes, hair flapping, they seemed a bright guarantee of life's flow.

Settlement children on the bank chased the boat as it swung away from shore into the centre channel, the daughters craning their necks as the father steered the next bend.

Middle Crevice

Snow. Sleet. Wind. Snow.

Lower Crevice

No dawn, only an extension of night, an overall milkiness several hours long waning into another night.

Yang Meeting

Brigands invade the valley and one of them cuts me open, guts me like a fish. The mountain explodes. Mountain Temple has been pierced on its east side by a huge uprooted tree and Spring Shrine has vanished.

In the storehouse a monk is eating alone, one who has never been friendly to me. When I speak to him, he shrugs and continues eating.

In my former life dreams didn't interest me and the large stories only mattered as backdrop against which we wrestled with our shaky existences. After the seals, the ferry, weeks of fog, I was escorted by Jake over the Iron Workers' Memorial Bridge, then flew across the ocean. That rift in my life so dark; I still can't assess what was seal, what was sea.

When I left the storehouse, I saw Song Wei near the river and hurried down through the gates and caught up to her on the bridge and followed her across and east into the steppeland of scrubby leafless brambles, tracking her wild leaps in the undisturbed snow till both of us were scrambling. "Wait!"

She stopped and faced me, her mouth open and hair blown loose, her breath rich with metal.

"Are you sick?"

"No. I am well."

"You shouldn't be here. It's dangerous."

With a quick gathering of clothes, she crouched to piss. Thin young bamboo poked through the snow, the leaves trembling. She stood, her belly a round taut curve. She turned to show me, to let me know, then refastened her clothes and laughed.

"Fine?" I said.

She nodded.

"I am in love with you."

Let me sit still and concentrate. A war is without significance unless it comes ashore. The boat was slow, sailing upstream. Probably, it had a well-caulked hull, and supplies for a while. The family had lost everything, but soon they'd be safe.

Hold and Support

The child was playing on the bridge deck with a wooden top while the father leaned, smoking, on the railing, the river charging and swirling just beneath their feet. They did not look at me.

I still don't know who this man is. He seems unconnected to the other villagers. He and his son arrived a month ago and we see them only occasionally. They keep to themselves, though I've seen the women give them food. I don't know where they sleep. This sighting comes the morning of my own son's birthday.

I woke up buoyed by joy — Song Wei's face, her eyes shining — then remembered the turmoil. And then I came upon the boy with his top, his narrow shoulders shifting as he made it spin and spin. Nothing can disturb the turning point if all else is fair, and if all is not fair disturbance will produce a wobble.

How can I blast out of the grand personal and live like a monk, each moment enough, despite mouth pain and the pull of Song Wei's eyes and the galloping signs of every imaginable disorder?

Stop the lens down and here's what you get: a darker world with sharper edges. I hated seeing myself in old footage — those boasting skinny nervous roles — so I avoided my early TV and movie work until I turned fifty. Then I watched each film, studied myself carefully to find the source of such youthful confidence and bravado.

Add time to the exposure and things are brighter and less stable: ghosts appear and buildings are less solid. Uphill the temple, surrounded by snow, snow thick on its roof, seems hefty and beautiful against the white mountain.

Frank's hands were shaking when he turned from releasing the timber to sound the midmorning bell, the tremor touching his whole frame before the echo reached the two of us on the mound above the spring. The noise prevented him from hearing my presence, but he was smiling as he shuffled over the trampled snow. I shouldn't have been there since no one must witness the bell struck, but I hadn't spoken to him in weeks. It was clamorous on the stone hill, the waves tolling back and forth across the valley, the yellow sky curdled. Below us, beyond the temple and storehouse, people were industrious, their lives visible just ahead of their bladelike bodies. How slowly they advanced in the pure land. How certainly.

"Frank."

"It's you. How was your trip?"

"The master is pleased."

"Good."

"How are you?"

"Good for an old guy. What d'you want?"

"Just to say hello."

"Well, then."

"There's trouble this winter."

"There is."

"May I shake your hand?"

"Of course." He thrust out his arm.

Through my fingers I felt the quick passage of life through his body. I set a finger on Back Ravine and his body undulated like a herringbone sky. Then I left him on his summit, and wound my way down the path to the spring. Splinters of ice surrounded the clear black water under the pine branches.

As I passed the temple, the silver pond blinded me, ducks skating the surface.

Frank is back in our world. He showed up in the storehouse, wild with talk, to register us with arched eyebrows and body tremors. He said the bell was no longer haunted. He had listened to the ghosts.

This afternoon he visited my corner of the storehouse to speak about America. He stood wavering, his hand light on my arm, gazing off into the books, and told me about a horse he once worked with, its smell, its threadbare coat and low voice, the thud of its heart.

"I am in love," I said.

He waved his hand. "What does the master know about the fighting?"

"He hasn't told us."

At the open door we listened to wind in the bamboo.

"That old lame horse locked her legs in front of me and her breath was sweet and loud, and she just died."

I walked him outside and watched him pick his way carefully uphill, and a short time later I heard the bell and saw my son walking away down a grey street. I loved and lost him. Imogen. Song Wei. Her baby. Frank's bells are a sonic support for all of this.

GATE OF ABUNDANCE

Another windstorm. Sporadic artillery at night. More boats. The valley a concoction of curving energies, the scorpion tail of spring, yang beating on yin, our fires guttering. Outside the storehouse door are epic clouds and on the bridge gulls, the first this winter, snow blowing in from the south. Last night I slept only a few hours, and woke amazed at the difference between my life now and my life then. My earliest adult memory is the one of being dropped off by my mother on the freeway, nothing in my pockets, sleeping in a ditch and waking at dawn covered in volcanic ash to birds and the quiet highway, believing the world dead, until the day's first traffic proved me wrong.

What is your earliest memory?

Surely not driving a Fiat sedan across a ravine on a derelict rail trestle one summer in shrub country north of the desert, a kid in the back seat, bumping over square timbers, a blue lake far below?

No. This was my small family. Before the real acting began, before you caught my eye, and before the raising of a child. Before debt and waiting and everything.

Floating Cleft

Each day was a single fluid gesture. Then when I realised you were real, I lay curled up on the floor for hours at a time in long depression, until there came a kind of itch only you could scratch, and the succession of great roles. But I never arrived where I believed I was going; your fault, audience member, witness, reader, judge. I'm still not where I think I am and I'm still reaching out to you.

My forebears shift uneasily among the valley ghosts and twisting storms, kicking stones in their panic. *Where are we?* This is water's home, I tell them. *And where is that?* Water's home is a warren of passages under the Milky Way. *The Milky Way?*

Snow hisses through the open doorway, melting on the platform, but not on the cold packed earth. Hypnotic snowflakes, fat white bees, slow and change direction. Dark birds flash among the flakes, vanish in the trees.

A child is missing. We must go out while the snow is still falling. Zhou Yiyuan came, half-crazy, to the storehouse, and said his sister was bleeding and she could not stand up and a child was lost, a girl, her footsteps before they were covered following the path beyond the temple.

I have been through North Gate and a little way up the mountain. Wind screaming in the trees. Huge gusts flinging snow and branches in our faces. We found the girl, not quite dead, almost buried in snow, under the heavy branch of a tree. Snow had blown against her back. Her face, turned to the base of the tree, was a bruise in all that white. What I once would have called a miracle. I helped carry her down to the village, exhilaration pumping my blood, where Zhou Yiyuan pressed my hands and said all was well.

Now the girl is sleeping and I can't feel my feet. I am very cold. When I shut my eyes there's an afterimage of swarming flakes. Song Wei is fine, the unborn baby too, although there was blood. So Zhou Yiyuan may be trusted. What a confluence of inexplicable things.

Listen to them singing, these villagers I know nothing about, as little as I know about the river. They say once it has entered the sea it ascends in a Great Goodbye, turning back the way it came as a river of stars.

OUTSIDE THE CROOK

The countryside is still. Then a bird lifts from a branch and flies through a spray of snow, and I find a white feather buried quill up. Shooting pains in my fingers from hauling disks of ice from the water barrels.

It must be beauty, what aches in my feet and hands. The pain is blood. Life coming slowly home. Another return. Stars in the sky, now through the trees, now starlight through the earth.

MIDDLE OF THE CROOK

The child has gone wild. After sleeping for a day, she vanished again, her tracks again leading through North Gate and up the mountain. The first rescue party had to return because this time she'd climbed quickly and had already gone beyond where we'd found her last. Monks with supplies and ropes were sent out but by late afternoon had not returned. The master gathered us above the temple as light faded, in the small cut between the bell mound and the gate. Footprints showed every monk's passage, a crazy history. At our feet, the spring was frozen and the land outside the gate looked dark and frightening.

"She is not lost," he said. He coughed for a moment. "There are valleys so steep and dark that only hermit monks have seen them." He waited, pale and silent, his robes flapping against his thin ankles. "These valleys can't be found by those who seek them."

This evening a half-moon lit the snow and I sat with Song Wei by the fire in her brother's shack, listening to distant guns, all guilt and fever because I did not join the searchers on the mountain; because I had not written to Imogen; because I had nothing to tell the master.

Now they say there are three fronts to the conflict, though a ceasefire is being negotiated, underwritten by the arrival of international forces. I remember it was in Kitsilano looking over to the North Shore that I became aware that mountains would outlast the fever (call it loneliness, call it heartbreak, call it commerce) that drives humans to the snowline.

ATTACHED BRANCH

The terraces are frozen. My fingers can't hold the pen. My left hand aches. It's a wrinkled and spotted thing with grey skin pouched at the knuckles. Snow has not fallen since the day before yesterday and the temperature has risen enough to thaw the south-facing fronts of the temple and storehouse. The pine forest is loud with shouting crows. By day the sun shines and great icicles hang from the roofs.

The party came home without the child. The village men are silent, the women praying. Two fresh monks have left to try to find her body before the next snowfall.

DOOR OF THE CORPOREAL SOUL

The master has retired to his room. All morning we worked outside, often glancing up toward Mountain Temple, expecting two exhausted figures, one burdened with the body of a child, then in the afternoon we began to catalogue the old records. Many are damaged by mice or by water. All the storehouse braziers were lit, despite the sun, and we luxuriated in the heat. My feet and hands at last felt warm.

This evening old monks recounted the ancient war between the North and South, when the last armies of the South were hunted by a union of Northern chieftains to a remote valley near the end of the empire, where they rallied around a young prince who had been wounded in the foot. Almost no one survived the long final battle, which took place nearby, though the location is widely contested.

Vital Region Shu

Warm wind howls all day, unnaturally steady. The master is sick. The girl is lost. We sense unbearable tension on the plains south. It is impossible to imagine spring. We have an unnameable debt to pay and warlords are parking their Jeeps on the far side of the bridge. *Another chorus of slamming car doors.*

The mind's complexity confounds me. Once, at a film festival in Italy, I walked out of a panel discussion, furious at the stupidity of the audience's questions (not yours, no, though you were certainly there) and their aggressive fawning, and went to the little kiosk in the square to buy cigarettes. On this soft blue day the tobacco, rich and dark, was the best I had ever tasted. I abandoned myself to the beautiful light and walked uphill from the piazza into the old town where, on a cliff above the harbour, was an ancient buttressed church, the drop sheer from its pitted south wall. The church door, at the top of a flight of worn stone steps, was scarred and crisscrossed with iron, an immense dam: each surface detail worthy of a lifetime's study. I stood, out of breath, finishing my third cigarette, festival organisers and fellow panellists in stuffy halls below me. What good is an assemblage of such moments, even if they fasten old habits to the present? What are these clues good for?

Buds on whipping branches, birds wheeling everywhere, and the villagers leaving hourly offerings at the shrines. What? What are we unready for?

Spirit Hall

The snow is thinner. The world is blown to shreds. One cannot live in a state of wind. Wind-anxiety feeds fear, and fear goes into rage, into revenge, unless it is channelled toward ritual and order. Let me concentrate. The heart is heavy, therefore the girl must be dead. Therefore the baby . . . Let me check my conscience. Let me reach below it into tarry shame. The girl broke free of the home valley that keeps us safe. We have not done enough. The world without Song Wei is grey, and snow, already thinner, cannot survive this salty wind. The oceans it came from are ordered into ranks of fishes waiting to be caught.

But then I see Song Wei on the path to East Shrine and know the girl will be recovered, the baby will live, and the white valley, smoke from our fires flying over the river, is only beautiful.

Yi Xi

Warm air melts the snow and flocks of birds swoop tree to tree, each trapezist precise as claws hit branch, snappy feet locking on. Then song. After the wind, another pair of monks went out to search for the wild child. I met Zhou Yiyuan this morning praying at Spring Shrine and joined my prayers to his.

The master's eyes were closed, his cheeks sunken. He was white and looked stern. The box Zhou had given him stood empty beside his bed. I sat with others watching his chest rise and fall, the light in the room altering, and wondered what the box contained. The air was thick with the scent of mushrooms and damp cloth and decay.

When I stepped from the master's room, I was weeping. Objects were indistinct — some kind of snow fog was slinking down the mountain from the high drifts. Song Wei called to me from the temple path. How ruddy her skin was! She touched both hands gently to her belly; the corners of her mouth twitched, and she bowed.

There was no colour or substance to the world, only this small dusky woman, her whole history at her back, simply dressed in a coarse brown coat, black and white trousers, black slippers. Opaque air and tears obliterated everything but this.

Diaphragm Pass

How will we approach the enterprise of riveting these flimsy remnants together? What role will be mine should war enter our valley? How will the world be safe again? What play is there between war and love? You have to play your part, you know. Fair is fair.

All countries provide the raw material for war, yet when I left the town I was born in I didn't know that every city's coffers contained stolen cash. I didn't know that the freedom implicit in love had been fought for by children. Can you tell me what ingredient is so precious or so dangerous it must be hidden generation after generation, swallowed if necessary?

Frank has organized watches on the bridge to check the villagers leaving and returning. Our paths are the same paths, yet not. My large intestine is a glittering fish fat with roe. On the ground north of the bridge rain mixes with ice and mud. There is no traffic on the road. Each time I cross the bridge, I own the bridge. When I leave River Mountain the water flows into my right side and out my left, and when I return, robes flapping against my body, the mountain reeling me in, the river pours into my left side and exits my right.

The south horizon beyond the open plain, so powerful and strange, is a gentle curve from on top of the mountain. My fingers on this page are real, just as the page is real, and something flickers outside, through the storehouse door, while I'm thinking of the place I was born, but I don't know if what flickers is precious or dangerous.

Imogen's a brief light circle. Once we were supposed to appear in the same film — well, I had several lines over four scenes; she was the star — but the project fell through. Song Wei is Song Wei. You are you (can you tell what is happening from your vantage point?) and this is nothing but play.

GATE OF THE ETHEREAL SOUL

Every few years a child goes missing and is never found. This has happened since people first settled the valley. Frank tells me there is a mountain upriver beyond the farms and plum orchards, and inside the mountain is a country where the climate is gentle, skies always clear, where descendants of the lost lead peaceful lives and cultivate their wide valleys, and wait for new children to arrive.

A few years ago the master told us we should act like boys. Our healing practice would only work, he told us, if we approached the gold pavilion (with a smile to the stranger at our side) as children.

YANG'S PRINCIPLE

Yesterday the monk who taught me the strange flows came to sit beside me. He waited until I finished writing and then, after a silence, began to talk about the master, then about himself, then about a sister he hadn't seen for forty winters, the letter he watched his father write to the master, his mother's hands fragrant with herbs, his uncle's puppet-god waving goodbye, the beautiful things he saw on his journey to the valley, did I think they had all been destroyed? As he talked I kept falling asleep. I couldn't stop my eyes from closing. His voice grew excited and then sad.

I was wakened by another monk when I was missed for the evening ceremony.

A tender-minded optimist cocooned in a dream. Adopted into the strange flow of the region's past. So monks are beginning to speak to one another. Often the topic is the master's health. Although the sun shines, warm on my face, there's a fresh breeze from the melting snow and I want Song Wei. I close my eyes and follow each breath.

WISHING HUT (PAPINI'S CORRIDOR)

Zhou Yiyuan was shouting, his body contorted, feet sliding on the icy ground outside the temple, his tongue creeping from his mouth, his face black. He wrinkled his nose and roared: "Wake and get ready! Taste the dragon fruit! You must plan for summer battle!"

STOMACH GRANARY

When you look at the same view day after day, with the seasons slowly shifting light so the edges of things blur then sharpen, with animals trotting or fluttering or swimming in and out of the scene, the boundary between who you are and who you might be begins to wobble. The library in the storehouse contains all naming and relationship processes. The ulcer on the inside of my cheek won't settle. A large explosion in the port has left many dead and wounded.

Too much, if you ask me. The earth can't swallow all this snow, then freezing rain, now blood. Even this library, normally the warmest corner of the storehouse, is bitter cold, and water has frozen in cracks across the floor.

When you spend too long in one place, one position, permanent cricks are inevitable. My legs have gone to sleep. Mould patterns on the pages map each day's imperceptible increase of light — is that the lost valley? the country in the mountain? If we could read desire we'd find the girl deep in the margin, where the binding's come unstuck.

It was wonderful to hold my son for the first time: a claiming and a being claimed. Such a beauty! And now, here I am trying to bite off my own toenails, looking for some adversary and finding instead my old face in a dark window. Perhaps my courage will rise again once sun strikes through and illuminates this room.

When I'm gone, when you are gone, when we're asleep, when pain has mocked every boundary, sunlit fog will swirl through the quiet valley and desire once again step forward with its tiny flourish.

VITALS GATE

Zhou Yiyuan is a dwarf who carries power and a dream and treats silence as an obstacle, yet when I look into his eyes there's tenderness loose in the chaos streaming up through his body. Because he believes himself thwarted, I don't know what to say to him. Dangerous, crazy and selfish. But perhaps he is a prophet and, if acknowledged, would be helpful.

ROOM OF AMBITION

Twice the taste of metal, horrible and familiar, from gritting my teeth; unpredictable leg twitches and counter-twitches. *Get up and do something!* No energy. Imogen haunts me, my reply to her letter stuck in my throat.

Womb Vitals

Better, after an hour at the bathhouse. Again, I couldn't find my pen when I came to write. Frank, back at work on his own story, called me over and showed me his dry speckled closed fists; I tapped one and it opened to produce the pen angled on his palm. I was overjoyed.

Sequence Edge

Horrible whistling mortar and gunfire all night, awake, crawling across frozen snow to squat shivering over the dark hole trying to vomit.

Yang Confluence

Walked the valley today, along the river and back. This side. West again. Exhausted. No words. No story. No sign of combatants. Our master is truculent and speechless.

Sinew Support

Why are you still here? I mean I'm stuck with you, I mean I'll keep it going as long as you're with me, to find things out, to find the fracture. And we will work the fracture together, right, despite differences and tension and stuckness, both of us challenging whatever pops loose. Abstractions and universals. We'll work them really hard, dig and drill deep with our inadequate tools — sorry, sorry, *my* inadequate tools — to analyze the bits and pieces.

   At the end, my wife and I were in despair but we had the boy. When we looked at him, he looked at us. But we were like those cave fish so long in darkness they no longer have eyes.

Support the Mountain

What we live, even a disguise, we become; so say what this is, I dare you. Assay meaning. Two rivers that won't meet? A boat and a dying horse?

Soaring Upward

Not going well. A battle unit passed upstream on a listing boat. There are things that cannot be shown in movies, things film can't catch: the almost foul smell of woodsmoke, my father's secret language, his words so quiet I believed them. Then another flicker of something — the glint of running water in a still meadow. Not meadow. Wrong continent. No matter how much is translated there's always the original to give things away.

Instep Yang

We're going down, without a flow chart, spreadsheet, or even simple accounting. Hold your breath. The mould map is unreadable. I'm old, in a life, here, and you are there, reading the dead, and the longer we go without direction the more frightened I am of losing you. The search for the little girl has been abandoned until the snow on the slopes melts. Edges are missing from every object. Candles are surrounded by a little fog. Beyond what light shows, is nothing but vague pallid shapes, nothing but the bell, as if it lives under a lake, and yet I would not wish a clearer world, not now; not for me the hard lines of bright spring, not yet, okay? Okay.

FEBRUARY

Kunlun Mountains

I SPEND 1/1, THE LUNAR NEW YEAR for the truly mad, recalling my roles in the tragedies. My first *Winter's Tale* (comedy, I know, but I died) I played Leontes' son Mamillius, ten years old, whispering in my mother's ear while my father raved; then I landed Titus Andronicus's son Lucius, Duncan's Donalbain, Polonius's son Laertes, and then (*another part of the forest*, jumpcut) I had a son of my own, and then I lose track. Always somebody's somebody until King Leontes in my second *Winter's Tale*, in which I blow everything in a paranoid cataclysm in the first act. Years later I wanted Lear but was offered Titus. "It's a bloody play," said the director, "but the beauty in it is timeless."

I went out to breathe in the full blue day and found Zhou Yiyuan crouched with both hands in muddy water. As he stood up, he pointed at the father and son on the bridge. "That man is a spy."

When they sauntered away we crossed the river and hiked into the south hills along slight paths, in and out of little valleys and gulleys, through dense shrubs and over deadfall, until we came to a grove of nut trees full of birds. Above us was a steep scree slope, unclimbable; behind, through a break in the foliage, the monastery was laid out under the cold sun, a toy town beneath the mountain. I had never seen the mountain so big, nor the monastery so compact and ordered and empty. Even the village seemed tidy, and the bridge was a perfectly angled dash across the winding river.

Zhou Yiyuan hitched his broad shoulders then turned to me. "I am going to show you something." He crossed to a huge tree and heaved himself into its low branches and let a long arm dangle. I grasped his hand and he swung me up and told me to go as high as I could and make myself secure. He crouched on a branch beneath me and closed his eyes.

Almost dark when two men slipped into the clearing; they were armed yet poorly dressed for the cold. With a grunt, Zhou Yiyuan dropped from the tree to the ground, the men shouted and skittered back, but he was quick.

"Look," he said. And showed me his wet knife. "Tell your master that we are safe for now. This leader has been eliminated."

The scientists say it's all chaos in the cosmos, that the deep structure of change is decay and corruption. We are reeled in like the last wild salmon for a taste of home and a glimpse of Eden, for one blissful moment heedless of our own messy natures, not even referencing the stars. Are we? Reeled in?

Hard frost on the ground. What happened in the nut grove? That taste of the ordered valley was instantly soiled. Supper today was one small fish, two dry black plums, a bowl of rice.

KNEELING SERVANT

East Shrine has burned. No one witnessed the fire, so far as we have discovered. It must have burned alone all night. This morning the smoking coals were still hot, although frost had reclaimed all but a perfect black circle. Because of the general dampness, it is hard to understand how a shrine could burn, and burn so completely, this time of year. Nothing of the contents remains. The master, when told, merely pursed his lips and turned his face away. He has not spoken, nor opened his eyes since the girl went wild. Nothing I say to him about the war will make any difference to anything.

Sunny day. My own exhaustion is all that engages my attention. When will he die? I always worried about losing things and lost many. Dropped cues and missed marks and lost lines. Many parts I read for. Lost my wife. Lost my son.

EXTENDING VESSEL

It is snowing, slow and steady. All.

GOLDEN GATE

It is snowing, slow and steady. All but the music of that. All but the chanting of prayers. How can it be the start of spring? At East Shrine there's only the smell of wet smoke. A thing is out of my system and it's time to introduce something new. A new creature, a baby struggling into her world, come down from her tree. I request a sign from the valley or from the mountain, yet when night closes in it's as you'd expect, quiet, cold.

CAPITAL BONE

Zhou Yiyuan has loosened more horror; he and I share another secret. Yet heavy snow prevents outside news from reaching us. This prolonged snowfall cuts us off and we are isolated, stranded. That and our measured routine, the keeping of festival days, our practice, keep us safe from the to and fro of armies.

The quotidian's a tunnel each of us squeezed through to get here, and we arrived just in time to face another threat.

We performed a corner-field ritual this morning; we had to dig down through the drifts to the earth. The corners must be recognized or the fields become infertile. The corners must be acknowledged, otherwise the crops are confused.

We vanished into the day's first hour to contend with fog and waist-high snow and incomplete dark, and skirted the great banks, followed the tracks of small animals, until we were in a corner of the upper east terrace, where we used the length of knotted rope to bisect the angle of the two walls and our fingers couldn't feel but somehow found the corner-point. And burned incense. It was cold, still. Nothing but smoke to send back to the world. No one to hear us, our chants like kids' fading voices. The armies were out there, planning losses, and we too, as we made our way to the next corner, would soon be smoke. At dawn a thick fog lay on top of the snow and it was already as though we did not exist.

Gong.

In the corners we seek disorientation. Monks escape the world to be re-introduced as a kind of ghost story. Once all the corners are claimed, it doesn't matter that the busy world — marine traffic, street traffic, air traffic — has scuffed our paths all the way back to where we started.

Dawn. In my mouth a quick taste of fresh wood fibre, and before me the face, no, the eyes of someone I loved. Ah. There's my own dog barking and my boy asleep in his cot. And, as I unlock the winter-door and enter, surprise surprise, there's nothing to tell, no more than the briefest exchange of looks. And, oh yes, gratitude.

Bundle Bone

In these non-days and milky nights, monks and villagers forget their separateness and act as a single wave, a unified energy, with no discernible line to divide the two communities. Our every breath takes us underground and up into heaven. Frank has called the guards from the bridge.

Above North Gate a hole in the snow has been discovered, a snow cave, an ice chamber, the shape and size of a child, yet empty.

Some union has taken place, is happening right now, this winter. A moon struck through with a blade of sun. Inevitable, I suppose, now the master is dying.

Foot Connected Valley

And yet we are so different. We are the landed, they the migrant tribe. We are vertical, they horizontal. From us they receive hospitality and protection. From them we receive a cold respect. Our master, the fortieth since the founding of the order, has said we require them because they are the quick cunning future, the glimmer on the horizon long after the day is done. Our old master is slowly turning, weighty enough, almost, to draw everything together. This new old blood, exiled and distilled and returned fresh, is a new drug, a new point of departure.

Of course it is Zhou Yiyuan's shout we hear in the night, and have been hearing since last summer, his voice sometimes low and murderous, other times high and keening. When I hear him now, I feel a kind of dawning comprehension, and imagine Song Wei somewhere down there asleep, the child inside her stretching out a hand.

"Are you ready?"

Without a word, he turned and I followed him, and we waded back to the nut trees, almost buried in snow, where he drew his blade and cut a single curved branch. "Bend this into a circle," he said. "The valley will be safe as long as your people and mine are related."

I remember when I shifted the focus of my sexual energy from women to splinters of light. When was that? No, no, it happened, briefly. My foreskin cracked and blistered, a dry envelope, inside which was a letter written on parchment. I put away the parchment (wish I had it now) and the head of my penis reddened and white cracks appeared and infection took hold.

Reaching Yin

My dear friend,

The master is unwell but wishes you to know that all in the valley is flowing, as it should for an aspect of the Great Transformation. We can always use money. We prepare for your presence, and expect you.

The snow is melting. Silent waveless eternity has washed up on these dripping branches, roofs, hats, noses, fingers. Streams have fed the field-pools and we are on the edge of a sea still as glass, the far trees upside down and the bridge only inches above the surface.

I dreamed of my son. He was a young man and I was furious at him for parking my car below the tide-line overnight and we looked out of the window in the morning and only the roof was showing.

At first it seemed to come from the far side of the lake, then from overhead, then was picked up by other voices throughout the valley. News of the master's death in the flight of arriving birds. Thousands descending at once into the arrow-straight bamboo, and waterfowl splashing, clearly joyous, in the middle of the lake.

My ex-wife died at winter solstice and I went to Emergency with my hurt hand and began to talk to strangers.

There's no question of the existence of these people, this place. And yet at night, when everyone is asleep, I believe I'm someone somewhere else. The habit's old, a preparation for the play, almost automatic; as instinctive as talking to you to stave off loneliness. You have been here as long as I have, and we both believe in the slow development of this unfinished work, the gradual entanglement of two communities by the shore of a lake that will drain at the end of winter.

Birdsong increases in volume through the day, then at sunset stops. A single sweet note from the temple bird perched on the warrior tree beyond the two gates. Above our heads the bell continues and men talk in quiet voices in the shadow of great events on the southern plain, while I stand at the edge, in the wings, holding on. I am a something, not-me. I can go crazy or grow wings. Wings from fins. Remember? This is why the valley is so fertile.

Gushing Spring   Yin Water

Sometimes I want to leave it out, the point heading, forget the Gregorian calendar, counting the days. Some mornings. But when I write the point it's like the first coffee of the day or a tiny green leaf. Or counting money. Spring anxiety opening all the vents along the kidney rivers, little gas jets dancing up. *Remember?* Remember. Light them quickly before everything in the past overshadows us and any spark will blow us sky-high.

I was sweeping slush from the edges of West Shrine when Zhou ran to me, breathless, wild. He wished to know who the new master would be.

What I said was unpremeditated. I asked how could another master enter a time like this? I said there would be no more masters.

In his incomprehension was something to pity. His pathetic look annihilated all my anchors and sky-hooks and I found nowhere still, nothing organised. And in the flood of memory and raw demands of the present the New Year started. Tree frogs started. A bullfrog, after hunger and home were solved, after a good sleep, began to moan.

Zhou backed away as if shamed. Before he loped down to the village he said we had something to finish.

Tonight we carry the master's body up the path to the death-cave.

BLAZING VALLEY

Hawk poised upon her real nest. Skip forward into night. The moment before meditation becomes sleep. Something is unwinding. Something . . . what?

SUPREME STREAM

Along the river is evidence of spring. The terraces are flooded, ready to plant. What else? Eerie silence to the south. Zhou Yiyuan and Song Wei inseparable.

A monk was bitten by a villager's dog, and women making brooms chased the dog away, and the monk sat abruptly on the path, bleeding. The wound in his calf was deep. I took him to the storehouse and bathed the punctures and bound his leg. We spoke quietly together about the villagers, even though his teeth were chattering, and he said he admired their toughness.

Song Wei is an astoundingly beautiful spirit who snares men to keep her visible. One version of what I saw south of the river last summer. Today her obsidian hair flew as she pursued the dog.

Great Bell

One morning my son came home crying, covered in scratches and bruises from crashing his toboggan, and I ran a bath and washed him, naked and shivering, in the morning sun, steam filling the little room.

And there was Song Wei, also naked, about to step into my bath, the light on her shoulders from the same sun, now a smear in frail cloud.

There are many approaches to the scene last summer: one a trapdoor beneath my feet, one a rope dangling from the flies, one a rent in the clouds so the pen throws a shadow on the page. Tendrils from the scene lead to drowning. What else? Long illness. Poison. Suffocation. Blood loss. Massive trauma. Insufficient. A slow dissolve. Insufficient. Cancer. Coronary. Shock. Despair. Insufficient.

The valley is not these words or what they describe, and words, even when they are not describing, or are describing what they are not describing, or trying to say what they can't say, words are not the mountain, the river or the temple. A book is a collection of ghosts, each day's entry a lattice of partial visions. If we examine together what has caught in the extended nervous system, note the burrs along the river of *qi*, threads and buttons and skin of this and that, a dry or moist accumulation, and turn a word into a sentence, perhaps, perhaps, we will be liberated. Ultimately, yes, finally, finally emptied of perspective.

Crossing the Iron Workers' Memorial Bridge with Jake. Each word a tower, a finished wonder. Iron Workers' Memorial Bridge. A mending beyond mending that tends to heartbreak, joy, love, community. But ask these to show. Request a demonstration, a little taste, and what you get will be familiar beyond belief, as insignificant as the ceiling of my room, the ceiling of your room. Remember the old bathroom wallpaper you tore off and found older paper beneath, and older paper beneath that, and beneath that fresh-picked roses? Or this. You sat in the tub and washed the one you loved, but when you turned to tell someone, she or he had gone.

The valley's like an accident, a mistake. Misalignment. Harmonic. Overtone. The fox, trotting the bounds of the monastery day in day out, his pace gradually slowed by age to a painful walk, his eyes still bright, stopped one night as though to let something large cross his path, and his head swung left before he died and fell.

Love will and will not be the beautiful woman climbing the hill each day at the same hour, skirting the forest and passing my hut, her steps measured as she flows uphill and turns east to the clearing where the shrine has burned, where new shoots define the circle of charred ground.

You read each word, but what's really going on? If logos begins the winding up, what attends the end-fuck, aside from a pain greater and deeper than any before, aside from a separation of this from that, aside from a fleeting seamless thisthat? To avoid a bridge of bones I write all night in the opposite direction.

(Remember the child from Ethiopia?) To the left of the disintegration there is a movement, a kind of animal homecoming.

There is no one but you to ask what is the purpose of all this, what have we come here to do, on whom are we spying and to whom should we report. We have information, a billion years' worth. Who waits to assemble our receipts?

Can we filter the vital from the insignificant and find a pattern, set the parameters by ancestral tradition, bring science to bear, raid the armoury? Oh and how much of ourselves should we donate to the mission?

Look. Smoke of returning gangs through the trees. Soon the river will find its summer banks. Zhou Yiyuan was right about summer war.

Meanwhile I dream of Imogen, and am troubled by Song Wei who climbs the hill every day; I watch for her to come but never see her descend. The master is dead.

WATER SPRING

Everything falls. Sunlight on the trees, on our shoulders. My sense of what I am doing, what we are doing. Something: I entered the master's cold room, forbidden, and in a corner found one of Zhou Yiyuan's carved figures. No one had been there since we lifted the master's body to the cave. I lay down on the floor and watched the dusty air above my head simmer in a shaft of sun. How busy were those few inches above the ground.

SHINING SEA

Eye in the dust, the world obliterated. The plains occupied. Footsteps approached, paused, then faded away and the room slept, mats, table, figure, pots dreaming, as outside came slowly in with its trees and sky.

This is where he slept and dreamed. No one would recognise the nest.

What happened was I entered my parents' room (down the monster corridor) to nourish their union and they hauled me in.

Now I'm building a nest for you to hatch your own sons and daughters in.

Hieros Gamos.

RETURNING CURRENT

Stood for an hour in the morning rain. *Iron Workers Memorial Bridge.*

No more meridians or points, no need in the New World. Night veiled the tops of trees. All the monks stood in the rain and mud after the chores of the day, facing north, the wishing tree to our left, the well to our right, warrior tree farther right. Neither rotting nor transforming. Frozen blue. Unused by anything that matters. Not alone, unless we are all alone. A fixity.

Zhou Yiyuan stopped by East Shrine. "Song Wei is by the river. Go."

"I don't need you to give her to me," I said.

EXCHANGE BELIEF

Mine was a small East Vancouver house, attended by a wife and son, though with more rooms than we were comfortable with. We grew thin and ravaged. Debt increased. No one got out intact.

I told Frank everything on a visit to his mound. He listened and picked his nose but said nothing.

Grass growing up through the water. The swaying patterns at odds with reflections. Disturbed and still. Budded plum trees shelter soggy monks in silent mourning. We cannot find colour yet, only greys.

When will the credits roll?

Guest House

Two men crossed the snowy bridge, a pathologist and an actor, headed by car to the Vancouver airport, chattering loudly from fear of loss and fear of being lost, since one must leave and the other stay, and then the goodbyes were quick.

Inanimate an intimation of animate. Growth everywhere: hill, field, bank. Winter, the season of loss, is leaving us. A master, his last year, going west.

Yin Valley

Every day we stand together for hours, exhausted. He is not with us, not with me. His spirit has gone to ground. A sturdy length of time must pass while one monk carries the prayer, the rest of us asleep on our feet.

Pubic Bone

No longer encumbered with a body, he slides from his cave through underground passages to appear in this ink and leave a muddy residue that clots the nib.

The cave was once a cinnabar mine and before that a human dwelling and before that a bear-den, according to claw marks high on the walls. Outside the entrance are green tailing hills; quicksilver still surfaces to gleam in ditches.

Our robes are filthy from trudging to and from the cave, several monks coughing. On the way to the storehouse I stopped at a water barrel and looked down at my face, the thick fur of algae vivid on the inner sides of the barrel. Villagers passed quietly behind me on their way from the storehouse, having assumed permission to borrow tools to work new terraces. They continued downhill, past all the monks standing in rows, heads bowed.

Later, I heard them working, farmers with one foot raised and an eye on the river and the far shore. Dressed simply, exalting in the mild wind, their hands steady. And now it's night, I hear them clacking stones in their fists and singing.

GREAT LUMINANCE

They live by the river, at risk, ready to escape. We live above the river, still trying to bind together the mountain's sky and the river's sea. I can't help thinking of what Zhou has said, that they are the privileged and we the homeless, we the newcomers and they the first people, even though we have been here seven hundred years and they arrived yesterday.

East of the valley the river bolts white into a rock throat to be released, after a mile of solitude, black and sullen on its last supple meanders through the green alluvial plain. I stood above the gorge with Song Wei, looking down from a height of twenty metres, dizzy a moment — would the water be deep should we step into air and join the torrent? On all fours I grasped the red path with spread fingers. Song Wei was laughing, her eyes dancing. "What is it?"

"I don't want to lose you."

Qi Cave

One side of the valley is about to leap into spring; the other threatens to collapse backward into winter. The bell sleeps and we cherish idleness. The paths, every puddle, stone and turn, are perfectly known. The sky does not exist at all since we do not look up. Ducks swim the expanded river, and geese returning from their southern campaigns splash-land among them. What in me resists all this? What in me wants to concentrate only on whether Imogen will or won't come at the end of summer? A lover, a goose. A fox in a girl's arms.

Four Completions

Two fish swimming in opposite directions. Big dipper aloft, stirring the pot all night, in a fizz of remote stars. I'm a boy, four thousand years old, aware of my Western alignment, hefting the lamb over the dying bull, then abandoning the lamb, and sitting down beside old Mercurius, old pickpocket, fishing the empty ocean, to wait for the sweet water-bearer to come sailing down.

What are we? The axiom of Maria: 3, 2, 1, blastoff! What are we? Trying to get to the bottom of things, Hierosgamos at the beginning? What a concept. We're so back-assward.

One warm day in the middle of June 1958 a crane stretched to complete the steel truss cantilever bridge across the Second Narrows between Vancouver and the North Shore, and the fifth anchor span was too heavy for the temporary arm holding it; seventy-nine workers fell and eighteen were drowned in Burrard Inlet, weighed down by their tool belts.

The monastery was established on the ruins of a mining village, one the Emperor destroyed because most of the workers and many villagers sickened and died. The Emperor himself lost his reason when the red ore was brought into the palace.

Middle Flow

Roosters call and answer, we answer the bell, and the living answer the dead. Cold fog steals through thin watery light, west to east, and then reverses as morning sun burns through.

Vitals Shu

What's hidden is poisonous when brought to light and I am infected.

Shang Bend

Truth is I need meat and sex, not this thin light. Couldn't get out of bed today. The tethers were so fucked up, I had to be cut loose by the orderlies. Pissed myself. One said, "Give it a break. Give it up." The other said, "Poor sod, he's had enough."

Spring is beginning, heralded by raucous coupling crows and great flocks of birds shifting through regions of sky — passerines in short flights around the trees, raptors navigating the high pale blue, and waterfowl beating and cavorting anywhere there's a puddle.

Stone Pass

Not only does the river flood its banks and retreat to a trickle, but sometimes it seems close to the mountain and sometimes far away. Last night's snowfall looks like a wave on the temple roof above the gold curve.

"Hold Stone Pass (kidney channel meeting penetrating vessel) to deal with fear, to deal with blood stasis in the uterus and to deal with infertility." I pressed the point on my own body. "Half a thumb out from the midline between the navel and lowest rib."

Song Wei and Zhou Yiyuan were listening.

"Liver is the time to choose. First house of the day, in fire's shadow. Now hold Gate of Hope, Liver-14, Cycle Gate, end of the twelve meridians, under the floating rib on the left side — here, find the branch of pain. These two points, you see, are close together, yin and yin, wood and water, anger and fear."

When I returned uphill to the lines of monks, the wind was blowing. I took my place and frozen bits of ice blew off the branches into our faces.

"I believe Zhou Yiyuan is trying to help us," I said.

Yin Metropolis

Bright mountain crow-crossed, blue-edged except for vapour. New parts are being handed out. Someone's being tortured. Someone's strapping on explosives. Someone's sharpening a machete. And we need a new master. No one is the obvious choice, of course. Soon we will know who we are. We'll keep our line orderly, keep our biographies and appointments up to date.

This morning on my way up the path to the temple I was stopped by the whooping taunts of owls. I paused to watch shadows crossing, silent looping lines among the dark trees. Two cat-faced owls stared at me from a low branch.

Open Valley

Spent the day with my dear parents, discussing football standings with Dad, showing him how to access the Internet — he cannot get the hang of the mouse — smelling something sweet on his breath, whiskey it was, mixed with aftershave, his smell. Dad's fingers were too big for the keyboard; he was worried about his coming surgery; Mother was in the doorway grinding her teeth and tremulous as a caught sparrow.

Then they went away and the night was dark. Snow fell, then moonlight, then more snow.

MARCH

I CAME TO RIVER MOUNTAIN TO BE SHOCKED. But shock, as I record these fat-budded trees and singing frogs, seems paltry. I smelled it then it was gone. For years I thought of nothing but the systems and rituals of the monastery, every day carrying what the master assigned me to carry. Nothing needed to happen, except in dreams, in meditation and through the meridians of the monks and farmers, and the river, as it had for millennia, brought all we required, season after season, while the mountain held us fast.

When a story or novel is turned into a film some essence, if not alchemised, is lost. Some mythic dimension is bartered for the moment. When experience is turned into writing the original must die. (But it's true, it's true: I gave the talk at theatre schools and acting workshops for years!) Alchemy requires yin and yang: a container, material, and process. The valley, these inhabitants, this work. When a player steps out of his role, the experiment is reduced to unstable elements. Since Imogen set foot in the valley all has been Eden, tree, serpent — God! I am the crack she has entered.

Ah, the sun breaks through the clouds and there's a goat in the cut where two paddies meet: we're on the right track.

Secret Gate

In the night Frank knocked on my door to tell me Zhou Yiyuan had killed a warlord from North Valley. He sat on his heels, looking off to one side. A mouse hurried about the room. "Your dwarf has been boasting. Apparently this summer there will be a terrifying conflict."

"What can we do?"

"You talk to him. Find out if he has any real power. There's something else." Frank was blinking with exhaustion. "The death master will arrive tomorrow."

"Who?"

"The death master."

"But who is he?"

"Temporary help." Frank showed his teeth.

"The new master?"

"He will spend nights in the cave, listening to the master's spirit."

"Then he will be the new master?"

My mother crosses the bridge to this side. She's nothing less than Quan Yin, Mother Mary dressed in cool blue light, her feet leaving tiny prints in the muddy snow. She says she's looking into less and less challenging roles; as always she carries her mug of black coffee, her list of worries, and is humming a pop song.

Corridor Climb

I trotted the polished track up to the nut grove in high-keyed orange light, and found Zhou Yiyuan waiting by the tree. Across the river smoke from the cave fire smudged the mountain. Below us, on the edge of the road, monks were gathered.

"What do you know about him?" said Zhou.

"Nothing."

A tremor to the air as the bus groaned and subsided. Around us a horizontal battle scroll unwound as the death master stepped down, warriors picking up their swords and flying at one another. Exhaust fumes attended the rattling vanishing bus as the monks led him to the bridge.

"This is promising," Zhou said. His eyes reflected the river's last light. "When will I meet this man?"

"What is happening out there?" I pointed south.

"The fighting has moved farther west."

The death master is middle-aged, tall and thin, with long black hair and an angular face with prominent bones. We monks faced him at the big gate at midnight.

"Have any of you read Kant?" he asked.

"Yes," I said.

"Of course."

We watched him parse the knotted string across the gate.

"What drives us isn't what we think," he said. "Reason always contradicts itself. By reason we always divide." He coiled the string and laughed; we all laughed.

The weather has turned dull and the temperature has dropped. We were shaking as we crossed the storehouse courtyard through blowing snow.

SPIRIT SEAL

All day preparations for the new era, half of us digging past fresh snow and soil and the others carrying frozen clay down to repair the floodwall. The minor shrine we pass reminds us that a monk hid there long ago and watched men battling across the valley.

SPIRIT RUINS

Thousands of ducks bank east on a warm breeze. An eagle flies overhead. First blossoms arrive along with news of distant battles and attacks and massacres. Beneath the mountain we wait: by the cave warming the death master's rice; guarding the bridge; in the boughs of the warrior tree; in a circle in the storehouse courtyard. Village women have hung flags from branches along the cave path.

The summer before last Imogen walked among us in a white dress and sandals and we stopped praying. We had no work. Behind her the grey river heaved in rising mist.

The briefer the exposure, the smaller the aperture, the higher the resolution of the image, and the greater the capacity for close-up; all depends on light and the lens. The lens through which this world is projected is finely scratched and the speakers can't handle the wind-in-bamboo frequencies.

SPIRIT STOREHOUSE

New ink for my pen and rain all morning, small quake last night. I must see Zhou. I must speak to the new master. Not yet. First talk to Frank. Something is shaking loose.

I watched a slow beetle crawl the edge of what must have seemed a vast sea. It's love manifest with a couple of options. Slide downhill, zigzag uphill, or move to a new neighbourhood. Remember a dog on each lawn, daily trips to the city, coyotes and gangs roaming in packs? Every beetle, of course, belongs in a hole or a tunnel. I'm describing her progress along the shore of the great lake to close the gap between us, something like that. As Imogen knows, written lines of dialogue precede the players; the Greek chorus is reborn in the vacillating subject-object of the movie theatre; epic boardroom confabulations ghost the domestic shadow box. Whatever, we seem determined to shift some raw blunt thing into the next cavity. At last the beetle disappeared inland, headed west.

Deeper and deeper we settle into sleep, as the ground shakes, the valley crumbles, and the river sweeps it all away. Imogen in her white summer dress was a living spirit; her body was clean lines and foam.

Likewise, the hole we dug today was deep and great in diameter, an almost perfectly round pond. We dug to water and kept going, but the hole was impossible to control, the sides caving constantly into brown water. Impossible to dig and yet we continued, all of us hurling spades of mud into the rainy air, until mud and spades were a blur and we couldn't raise another drop. Swans peered at us over the edge and shrikes called back and forth overhead and the river ran away mocking.

Of course, such struggle is customary, and bodies are obliquely familiar, like daylight. Who the hell should I consult?

MIDDLE ELEGANCE

My father gave me his wallet and watch to look after while he had his surgery and in the wallet was a picture of my mother taken on their honeymoon. Black and white, dogeared, private. She's in a doorway, facing the street, one toe dangling over the threshold. He had the tumour removed from his colon and a stoma opened in his belly to take the colostomy bag. He told me he'd visited his own father in hospital when I was six or seven. It wasn't far from where he worked and he'd drop in every evening on his way home for a half-hour chat until his dad died.

Last night, shy of sleep, I kept watch with the new master over the body in the cave. The old master, with his round dry face and downturned mouth, lay on the cold packed dirt, his gentle brown eyes and shock-white hair gone away.

The temperature has risen and decay lingered at the cave mouth. The new master told me he had hiked the lower mountain paths.

"Yes?"

"Have you often been to the top?"

"Not often."

"Have you seen the Rockies?"

"Yes."

He was so happy to hear this. His fingers, long and thin, twined in his lap. "Tell me about the Rockies."

My sister and I took turns with our father, back and forth across the country, to and from the hospital, shepherding our fractious mother, until the end. What amazed me at his death was the realisation that he had always been with me, even though I'd taken him for granted.

Signs of spring grow more blatant. Zhou Yiyuan and Song Wei exhibit a nervous restlessness. Change, major change, seems unavoidable.

SHU MANSION

My parents again, sightseers, are rambling through the valley, taking in the bridge, the storehouse, the shrines, six views of the mountain, five views of the river. I stumble into them at the high garden wall.

They do not speak, but stand together at the gate, white-haired and inconceivably dear, nodding their heads at the first plum blossoms, affected and puzzled that they cannot enter. They do not understand this life. What they did, deliberately or accidentally, to nudge me into the world, we will not do here. My mother talks about the ocean. She says the sea is all she cares about now. "I made mistakes," she says. "I fucked up. I had a lot of fun but I was mostly miscast."

Dad says, "Preston North End one, Liverpool nil, at Anfield." Unlikely.

My mum's a nervy wave clattering onto a pebble beach. Dad's a disappointed fan. But at least here they don't have to boost their relationship.

Sky Pond   Yin Fire

The new master looked like a tall woman as he stilted among the villagers, slowly through the heavy rain, while they ran bandy-legged, sloshing mud. I was in anguish when he stopped to talk to Zhou and Song and she looked up toward the mountain, toward my hut, where the rain screened me and a woodpecker caught my attention with his wavy flight. He is in his forties, younger than I thought, with a slight tremor in his long hands. Present in him is clarity, and he has a kind face, and people have loved him, and he has loved them.

He asked me to meet him at the cave and I took the path after the violent afternoon rain, sunset thickening the clouds. Outside the cave steam rose and on the bushes sticky leaves were beginning to unfurl.

HEAVENLY SPRING

He seemed surprised when I told him that Zhou Yiyuan might not be trustworthy.

"You know him well?" he asked.

Mist over the river and fields. Black clouds to the south. Both of us breathless.

A coil of smoke rose from the fire outside the cave where the youngest monk, still a boy, was cooking rice. This boy was so new, so smooth; his ears were fresh and his neck a pure delicate column. I recognised a son turning at his father's voice: he was lost in the new master's clear eyes. Greenfinches chattered back and forth.

Then there was a crashing in the trees below us and an old brown bear swarmed up to the boy's fire. Shocked, the three of us scrambled deeper into the cave; the bear upset the rice pot. Groggy, his smell sharp, he stepped into the cave and huffed.

"Make noise," I said.

"He is a cloud bear," said the new master.

The bear nosed the master's stiff body then, as we all yelled, he strode from the cave downhill and into the bamboo and I rushed after him along the cave path, sun glancing off the tops of trees, and he stopped and turned.

The cloud bear was the old master, the river twisting beneath his outstretched claws, and when he vanished I returned, shuddering, to make an offering. The smoke from the little fire still rising into the sky.

"We should have let him have one of the master's arms," said the new master. "You should have given him your arm," he said to the boy. "That's all the cloud bear wanted."

Marsh at the Crook

My parents stood outside the garden, close to the locked gate.

"What's in there?" said my dad.

"Flowers and trees."

"Likely."

"Winding paths and a lake in the middle."

"Very believable. You haven't been in there, have you?"

"Gardeners repairing fences."

"What fences?"

"For beans to climb."

My own dear parents stepping down the incline of short grass to the large flat stones that mark the west limit of our grounds.

This afternoon Frank and I tried to get the old crane on the ruined dock working; the icy wind was full of disinterested birds. Song Wei walked by us; rust flaked from the threaded nut as I forced it, the village men laughing, my mouth full of iron bolts.

XI-Cleft Gate

"The hills are dark with the sun behind them," said the master. "But the river shines."

We were gathered outside the temple door. Crows darkened the late afternoon, flying west to roost. Below them, on the horizon, was chill blue weather, electrical storms, earthquakes, disorder plus an underworld, trouble on the south plains.

"Our hill gives an unimpeded view of the valley and the mountain guards our back. There can be no approach in numbers, except by the river. So we are safe."

His hand was bandaged. He had burned his fingers on the last of the cave fires. Left hand, the palps of two fingers, large intestine and pericardium. Hammer and tongue, metal and fire. Constitutionally, he's an earth being.

"What have you heard in the cave?" said Frank.

"You are a bellringer, yes? We will go and wash off this mud." And he led us down through the plums to the bathhouse.

We have begun to compete for his attention.

The village children, invisible in silver rain, shrieked.

The bus still flashes upstream twice a day. One warm evening Imogen will alight. Chances are fair. Although she has not responded to my letter, she has sent money. Since the end of summer, we've been hanging fire, our work here a perpetual antebellum promise, nothing finished nothing begun.

Messenger Between

Skirting the fields this morning I found deafening birdsong and Song Wei in the middle of a rice paddy, her robe tied around her bulging waist, dancing head down amid flying water and ice crystals and mud while a hawk circled above, and *What have we done* to isolate ourselves from such joy, in the name of the family, in the name of good deeds, in the name of the earth, *Guilty as sin*, and I circled the paddy, to be on the safe side, to see things from all angles, to listen. *She is drop dead, she is a fox.* Song Wei dancing in the rice paddy while the hawk circled above.

Meditation is desire. Without sex, the foreskin shrivels, dries out, till it's a fragment, a pink birthday balloon lost in a ditch, a baked rubber gasket, cracked leather button, gritty chewing gum. My penis feels like a snake too old to shed its skin, though I will piss every day until my breath stops. Kidney, old secret best friend, hold your tongue in darkness. I won't stop drinking. I will give you rivers and rivers to mark the route we took, including detours and resting places and everywhere we spent the night, shivering. (Liver, guide my anger home.)

Inner Pass

Slept the night right through without waking. At dawn went to the river to watch the ducks roll and play with light and current's inflection, the clarity of the water. The dotted surface meant nothing to the little ducks making a journey downstream beneath a sudden rain.

We worked on one another in the big room west side of the storehouse, only our breathing and rain on the roof, gusts of wind, for company. A fish squirming against the flow — my finger on a point, gall bladder fire — nudged the surface. Surface: dynamic witness. A hawk screamed. The bamboo stick that held the shutter open snapped and except for my fingers and this monk lying on his mat all was in motion. *Picaresque.* Ah. That word I keep losing. The storehouse, closed, was complete — all planets and stars trapped inside — so we monks could complete our work, each bent over another.

Here's the monk's story: One day the boy ran to the edge of his town, cast his eyes in each direction and reeled in nothing but blowing dirt. But wait: to the west was a gathering of mountains and a dirt devil spun at his feet and his life depended on what he chose, though now I was responsible for the way it would go next.

GREAT MOUND

Before the war my father fished Ullswater in the Lake District. He set nightlines for eels. He slept in a feather bed in the attic of his aunt's hotel and got up before dawn to check the lines and to row city men out into the lake. As they fished, he tied flies and readied the spare rod. And even though the beck by the hotel ran grey from the tailings of a lead mine high in the hills, there were buckets of eels and the businessmen were always able to catch several trout in an hour. By the 1960s the lake was empty.

Today we burned the old master's clothes in a ceremony to release spring. They blackened slowly, creating a lot of smoke, because spring must creep in, otherwise flooding would cause damage. Our clothes used to be made by women from a village in North Valley and were called "winter-spun." Now they are produced in a small factory in the port. The old monks say the colours are brighter but the material is not as warm as it used to be. A smoke river followed the flight of geese across the sky. Our feather design is still reflected high above in these spreading clouds.

This transition from death master to new master, accomplished in the cave through ancestral agency, is a process of weaving surface and depth. I think it's right for me to be apart from others of my kind and to be here, shocked or not, but soon it may be necessary for me to live alone. There are threads connecting all things, it's true, but the death of our master has brought cataclysm and uncertainty into high relief, and solitude may be the only way to tease a way through. What d'you think? My solitude might be useful to others — holding a door open — in a way I've never thought of before.

PALACE OF TOIL, GHOST CAVE

After the middle of the night. In the darkest part of the wood. Zhou bent the branch into a circle and we stretched the skin over it. An owl called. I had to pull off my left shoe to scratch the itch inside my big toe. *Dadun* Liver-1. Jing well point and wood point of the liver channel. Did Large Hill itch because of the hour? Did I have an overabundance of earth? I showed Zhou the centre of my palm, Pericardium-8, ghost cave, fire point, good for fever.

He helped me fasten the skin to the drum frame, warned me not to sound it. "This master has evolved from winter," he said. "What is his purpose?"

"I don't know."

It was dawn by the time we were back across the river. Song Wei greeted us at the bridge in a flying gown. Angry eyes and brand new green wings.

CENTRAL SURGE

Count the breaths it takes to climb from the storehouse to the temple. One hour's meditation equals seventy-two inhalations, seventy-two exhalations. A small olive-coloured bird has fallen in love with the Quan Yin statue — the past few days it has been fluttering around Quan Yin's face, trying to penetrate her eyes. Counting my breaths downhill. The new master, the temple, the storehouse, the gates, the walled garden, the warrior tree — no matter how many I counted, the number seemed unreasonable. Like the surface of the well, the drum was still.

Rushing Pass   Yang Fire

Voices entered our heads as we meditated: goats on the temple path, rain on our shoulders, the small cries of blossoms, smoke from cooking fires, angry shouts. Yet our words were gentle words.

WATER DOOR

Two boys swam out to rescue a cat in a tree collapsed across the river. They in turn required saving. Everyone in high spirits.

Central Islet

The master has agreed to accept the boys. Three of us accompanied him down to the village where the women paused in their work and men came out of their makeshift huts. After a few minutes' silent greeting, the master explained that the boys would begin their training right away. The boys laughed and sneezed as he described the flows. The men drifted back inside their warm nests and the mothers touched their sons' foreheads, and then we followed the master to the temple where he took their fingers and traced a journey on his own body. The boys grew bored then sleepy, their eyes closing late in the afternoon. They would never again be so full of promise.

I made my way back to the village to see Song Wei. She was alone, near where the children were playing. One hundred steps took me across the bridge. This count had never happened before so I retraced my steps and the count was one hundred again. She pretended not to see me going back and forth.

I remember my son sobbing all night after finding out he'd failed the art school entrance requirements. He was twelve and knew his life had altered course. I bought for him a detailed model of a World War II Spitfire, complete with ground crew, but he built instead a tiny replica of the acropolis and my wife sliced off the tip of her finger cutting dowel for the pillars.

On the wall of my hut is Zhou's stag skin sewn onto its circular nut-branch. The pulse stored under the skin.

Yang Pool

Everything is possible. You love a person or you love no one. Lives begin and end in a rough instant or they never get started. God is alive in the world or not real. The middle of the ballpark is just that, minus the guesswork. You sit or stand, unaware of breathing, until you forget to breathe. Any number of zeros, without a prefix, accounts for the dead. Forever travels in small groups, never more than six. There are twelve types of chaos.

The master waited for me by the cave and turned in silence and I followed him up the path to Spring Shrine. We crouched and wet our mouths.

"It has been some years since I was last here," he said.

"You have been here before, though."

"Yes. When I was a boy I studied here." He gestured toward North Gate. "I have never climbed all the way up the mountain." We waited together as if for a signal. Eventually he raised his head and spoke in a quiet voice. "Once this mountain was under an old sea, and our sea was over another land."

A goat screamed from across the valley.

"Is that Zhou Yiyuan," he said, "or Zhou Yiyuan killing somebody?" He smiled.

"He says we will lose everything. He says it is inevitable."

"What does he want?"

"I don't know."

Time was preparing an evening meal. A family reunion feast. The familiar bend in the river hit me with force. It stunned me. I paused on the bank and didn't know whether I was east or west of the monastery. The birds fell all at once silent, as if exhausted, or as if working at something fiercer than song, shaping an internal storm that might carry them away unless they clutched their branches tight. With similar force the river flowed. Tonight the quiet was the absence of what we did, our own song and dance — monastery, well, garden, gates, bridge — quiet that would only expand with what we tried to do in darkness.

Toward the end of my marriage I was capable only of endless words. Each time we stopped talking, I struggled madly for the next words, knowing my wife only wanted more words, just as I longed for hers. She kept saying she wanted me to listen, and I said I was listening, and she said no, I was listening to the world as if it did not contain her.

When people fall out of love, they push each other around. We were trying so hard. But I did not know, really, what she wanted, and I didn't even think about what our son, alone in his room, wanted.

Outer Pass

The master gathered us at the temple. "At the top of the mountain," he said, "lives a young man who every moment changes to suit the moment's needs. He can't be seen because he adapts so quickly. He is just out of adolescence, and wild. When he runs, his legs and arms are untidy. His need for where he's going is breathtaking."

Frank sat with a blanket round his shoulders, leading the chanting.

"The connection between us and the boy on the mountain will aid the success of human projects all over the world," the master said.

"He is not sure what is going to happen," said Frank.

I asked Zhou Yiyuan when I should beat the drum. He said I would know.

"The master wants to know what you want."

"We travel the same path but in opposite directions."

My over-charged system found the furniture rearranged, the right people in the wrong place, morals askew, exaltation and paranoia. Stage sickness call it, instinct locked into a vicious loop. I dried.

Zhou Yiyuan cackled; he crouched, grasped a fistful of dirt and tossed it west.

The reason I went to theatre school and then found an agent and then jobs, stage and screen, was to create a face and body acceptable to the world, but ultimately I was unacceptable to myself. I couldn't find the emotion and couldn't hold the line and couldn't time a response, and that spelled the end, that ended the spell.

River Mountain's one-point approach adjusted my pattern and (*he sold his red Lotus and voluntarily paid a retroactive carbon tax*) swept away my audience, neighbours and the dead, like so many brilliant leaves, and soon, at the end of my life-long skid, I will find myself toothless on a grand alluvial plain, unbelievably vast, one-third the planet, say. Just wait.

Like the birds or the cat or the boys, I must cling to what I know: the way the son grows into the father will determine how the father will lead or leave his son.

I would like to play the boy on the mountain. I'd look forward to his scenes, in the middle act, with Nietzsche and Parmenides, not to mention the wild girl. This would help me to puzzle out everything so I can tell Imogen when she comes. If reason is driven by desire, then lust accrues around a kernel of truth.

BRANCH DITCH

This is my place for now, to conjure from the mists lung and heart, river as drainage ditch, and rain to nourish the black pond. I hope one day to see my son; perhaps he will fly into the valley as clumsily as I once stuttered past my father's and mother's deaths. My own waits down a crooked lane through windswept leaves, the broom fallen aside, a breeze in the long grass, no one to call.

ANCESTRAL MEETING

Amid many broken things. Branches. Worm casts. An upturned beetle.

THREE YANG SPIN

I have found a stone more like a fish with glittering eyes than an egg, though I thought of placing it in a nest built this time of twigs and twine and lined with soft dry grass. I have been watching crows to improve my engineering skills. This kind of attention is free of learning, free of knowledge. And they laugh at me.

FOUR RIVERS

Such self-deceit and pride. All I do is human, if a million years old, only the latest version of animal. I'm just another person holding aloft the next cruel or tender act to the night sky and opening his fingers. This notation measures my humanness.

Consider the distance from sky to earth and the distance from the top of your head to your chin. Consider low sun purring along the edges of trunks, branches, roofs and gates, and the constantly shifting sparks on a river. Childhood in each cell, and that death room down the crooked lane, from which you will not rise.

I remember being a boy sick in bed with a cold, home from school, the radio on, hearing distinct footsteps on the street, a barking dog . . . ultimately consumed by the smell of Dad returned late from work at twilight to say night-night before it got utterly dark.

Sky Well

This day, sunny with perfume, loud with birdsong, I walked to the river and along, taking my time, and found the lakes shrinking. After months of grey the sky was sublime — the inside of a gorgeous bowl — although the coldness of night and winter were sulking somewhere behind the light. Meanwhile I study the drum, circle and skin.

Clear Cold Abyss

We left the river hours ago and came through the bamboo, past the cave, by forest path to North Gate, and climbed steadily through the evergreens, and were in snow nearly to the tree line. The new master strode ahead of us. We were to discover the doorway between physical and spiritual passion, he told us. We must release our thoughts. There were four stages to all human endeavours, he told us. This uphill walk, for instance. First the scrambling feverish hurly-burly dyslexic beginning, all of us panting and staggering, calling for rest. Then our rhythmic rolling gait through synchronous slips of fragile nature. He stopped and grinned. "Soon," he said, "will come the weary dogged dreamy struggle. And last the terrible stumbling climb. But we will not reach the top today.

"How do we achieve knowledge?" he asked.

The two boys at his feet adored him.

"By tracing the channels," one said.

"How often?"

"Four times a day."

"Why do locals leave food near the spring?"

"For the boy on the mountain!"

"What is the point to save the world?"

"The mountain!"

"Let's go." He took each by the hand. "Let's find a dry place for the night."

I held the question I wanted to ask, and found beneath a tree the broken blue shell of an egg and set it on a mossy stone. This secretive act reminded me of something I've been trying to do since the fall. My nest-building was a kind of self-promise.

Below us the river was red with ore stirred in high streams. The mountaintop, pure white, looked near enough to leap over. I closed my eyes and flew over the summit into the next valley as easily as I once flew through life.

Dispersing Riverbed

The master looked at me for a long time. We were above the tree line, watching the sunrise and listening to the bell ringing far below, our breath pluming.

"Zhou Yiyuan has been to see me," he said. "You are in some trouble. Please think of one word a day for four days, then bring them to me."

Upper Arm Meeting

If experience is assimilation — adaptive process born of instinct — then choice is a mill whose flour is safety. But what words?

Shoulder Crevice

Knot.

APRIL

SKY CREVICE

Story.

WINDOW OF HEAVEN

Chain.

WIND SCREEN

Nest.

SPASM VESSEL

"I like your words." He smiled and the valley was like a small room. "Zhou Yiyuan, Song Wei, yourself, and me."

My first dog, a white poodle called Larry, wandered through the crowd of visitors and the few monks and villagers remaining, and I hadn't the breath or voice to call out, though I wanted his eyes on me again. People thronged outside and inside the storehouse, and there was barely space this side of the bridge to turn around, and we all shuffled slowly uphill toward the temple, the faces near me preoccupied and sad, as more strangers stepped ashore from barge-like boats, and between the river and the mountain was an ocean of new people, and Larry was nowhere to be seen.

At my confusion, the master leaned close and smoothed his hands through the air. He put his arm around my shoulder and led me to the well and drew a cup of water.

The day was warm and a haze of cotton fuzz flew above our heads, while swifts danced along the river that swept pollen through farmland and a number of towns, past a city and into the sea. Perhaps there was no more than that to observe, nothing further to say. Merely a daydream and a redistribution of materials.

"Zhou Yiyuan commands the respect of two warlords," he said. "For this reason he has the ear of the government, though he is not trusted. His agenda is unclear and his methods unpredictable. Did you know his sister is a shaman?"

I nodded.

"However, he is unafraid and tireless and has been useful to the military when conventional approaches have been exhausted."

"His people originated here," I said.

"That is not true. He does not belong to these people."

"He told me you and he were on the same path but going in opposite directions."

"We are both eccentric," the master said. "What does he want?"

"I don't know."

We sipped water from the deep blue cup, passing it back and forth.

"The old master asked me to find the point to heal the valley," I said. "Zhou Yiyuan showed me the point."

"Ah. Tell me, please."

"It is across the river."

He shook his head. "Not the mountain?"

"No."

"No," he said. "How did he show you?"

I lay on my back on a rocky outcrop above the cave where the bear had come snuffling and watched the clouds. One over, one under, one faster, one slower. Redistribution of vapour. I dreamed the land was crumbling, these rocks about to fall into a cavern under the monastery, the earth already fissured with parallel cracks, and woke with late sun on my face.

So I fetched my materials from the corner of West Shrine out into the last sunshine. I have told the master about the rape and the killing but not about my attachment to Song Wei. What does it signify? What would it signify if three points — the fallen tree, the nut tree, and Leopard Pass — were connected? The pen moves all by itself to record signs — reflected light, a twitchy yellow smell, a dog's bark — as though they are beings with distinct lives.

Skull Rest

The villagers sweep the graves of relations who have died in our valley. At a pause in our chanting by the cave, we listen to their wavery singing. A bird is calling *clear-and-bright, clear-and-bright*. Since I have lost my country and countryside, my parents and wife, I own all rivers, all mountains.

Young Angle

The villagers are busy planting. *This slip of green belongs exactly here. This is mine . . . this is mine to give to you . . . this is yours . . .* Why is possession a comforting thing? Why did I give up one place for another, one relationship for another? Do possession and comfort have no meaning without loss?

"There are answers and accidents," the master said, "the facts and the wobble. Answers are plentiful. We fill our talk with reasons. And since familiarity produces a kind of ownership, we are faithful to faithful answers. If you don't change your life, accident will."

"Leap while the leaping is good?" said Frank.

The master laughed. Between him and Frank ideas popped up like ducks, their beaks cranked with fish or snakes from the weedy depths. We monks sat in the courtyard and listened, unless he asked one of us a question.

"The valley I've lived in all these years is changing," said Frank. "There are young trees where the marsh has receded, and old trees have been cut down. Monks have died, and young men have taken their place. My old master has died; you have arrived."

Standing to stretch, fingers soothing kidneys, I witnessed some fussing thing catch a jagged black line — broken branch, crow — the gist of what they were saying. The gist I needed to record. Because I'm keeping secrets.

Below us the elder women worked together, crouching low, their chins jutting. We plant a higher terrace, while the women peck at the soil and at noon hide chattering in the reeds on the bank of the sparkling river, dipping fingers into wooden bowls. All afternoon crows splashed in the puddles.

"Mr. Western Philosophy," the master said. "Please tell us about passion."

Above us, on the storehouse roof, pigeons rehearsed entrances and exits, and the sky held faint grey striations, a hint of gold where the sun would set. A hundred ducks took off from the lake fields and the women angled their faces and laughed. The light off their eyes diminished the river light.

EAR GATE

"Why did you come here?" the master asked.
    "My wife left me and then died and I lost touch with my son."
    "Why are you still here?"
    "I don't think I could live in a city again."
    "Why not?"
    "Too many people, too many cars. Too much of everything."
    "Not unlike this place," he said. "Hold Leg Three Miles, both knees, to clear fire and steady your spirit."
    We bent together under the warrior tree clutching our knees.
    He's right. It's the same here. Refugees drift downstream, more and more every week, and when I see hurt children, even one child, my knees weaken. Children loosen my ribs: the village kids, the youngest monks, those wild-eyed kids passing east on boats or rafts.
    So we stood holding Leg Three Miles and gathered earth through the gates of our knees. Anything might happen. No one was safe in the wilderness. There was only one big story with two strands: home, migration.

EAR HARMONY CREVICE

Woken by a bird shouting like an American robin, that sad frantic song. I dressed and went out to listen. A monk was wandering under the plum trees near the bathhouse in a storm of white petals; he stopped still on a white shining dais beside a dark trunk. He too was listening. South, under a grey sky, the bridge deck was wet, its hills dotted with white and pink. Overhanging the river, the willows were fresh green. I had to squint to recognise villagers in the middle distance. A twang: the narrow leather back of a hummingbird at a flowering current. The noise of equipment. Frank telling the new boys how to work the bobcat.

Silk Bamboo Hollow

Zhou Yiyuan and Song Wei stood side by side on the bridge watching a piece of torn red cloth tied to the railing, flapping in the wind. A heron called from the tall tree near the road. Song's belly was full and round and she cradled it in her hands. Brother and sister, heads bowed, studied the red cloth as it shivered, rippled and convulsed, its end secured in a fat knot. A barge floated under their feet, children curled asleep on the rough boards, while their mothers huddled under blankets and looked out and the fathers dipped poles and oars to keep midstream. Zhou raised his hands into the sky. He might be Song's burly misshapen son. The day was one capacious grey cloud, gulls soaring high against its underlay.

Pupil Crevice   Yang Wood

There you are, right behind me. You used to be in front, to the side. Remember that local play in Victoria, my last performance, breaking the fourth wall? I broke my hand, my writing hand, the next day. My ex-wife had just died. I didn't mean to hurt it, but wanted to protect my body from hitting the cement. An accident. I'd been doing the same thing — leaping the steps from the back door — for weeks; she'd told me I'd break my back; "For God's sake, how old are you?" Then I was on the ferry, replaced by an understudy, in mourning, one hand in a cast, free fingers tapping the keyboard, glancing out of the window at the sleek seal breaking the surface of Active Pass.

"I don't want to repeat myself," I told the master. "I don't want to keep doing the same thing."

"Every day is repetition," he said. "Repetition helps us remember the points. We are in a major flow. You were an actor. You know repetition is rehearsal."

This sent me back to you, my old construction, my old friend. Every rehearsal, as it smoothes the snags and burrs of a production, invents a variation, subtle or coarse; every rehearsal digs a hole, shears a few molecules from the stage, and starts something fresh as it recycles the old tropes. What do you think? You of all people must know this! The trouble with performance, and this monastery — and every camp, prison, sanatorium, terminal, institution — is that it reminds us of what we have lost. I loved my fellow actors, but you only loved who they played. You are like this pebble. I will never lose it. There you are, little shiner, little one. I'm not going to let you go. Ever.

Hearing Laughter

The deeper my son sank, the less detail and texture of his life I saw. I couldn't even imagine his life. I worried about him, put off contact. I couldn't face or imagine what might happen to him. What possible value was speculation, and what use was imagination, what use? And what did I do? It's one thing to embark on an esoteric apprenticeship, fulfil the requirements, years later to emerge a prophet or healer, light sparking from every orifice, it's another to give up on a boy.

Upper Pass

I've got you now, Mother, you won't get away this time. I was a better actor than you because you fucked around and I kept that part of my life under control. In the end it was my success kept you fed, kept you housed, right? You always said you wanted us to cosy up together, the two of us, buttered bagel cut in half, pack of smokes, brace of nice gin fizzes, film credits for me, for you TV, one of us drunk and the other stoned, neither of us good listeners. I can't remember a time when you weren't rushing through spilt perfume, busted zipper, the studio bloody with screaming. *Take it easy, Ma. Calm down.* After all, you got what you deserved after working so hard, hiding your need for approval. Alzheimer's and a violent death. Ta da! Now we're equal, equally forgotten. That's it. I won't talk to you anymore. We're finished. You're forgiven.

Jaw Serenity

The man returned from a long shoot to find his wife gone and several changes to the house: blinds on all the windows, new locks on the doors, and a hot tub in the back yard filled with snow. So tempted to smash a window to see what else. Wasn't there supposed to be less after a catastrophe? It's a lot of work, memory, the jerk to pull the logjam loose or the slow steady tow to free tree after tree, and after the initial thrill of clearing the channel, there's only flow and the end of a season, end of a run. I'm no longer innocent, but I'm not guilty. I'm beginning to confuse my dad's life with my own, though his absences were real and had nothing to do with acting. What do I know? I want a new window on my own passage from childhood to adolescence, from the seesaw to the first ejaculation, that basic leap. Because I forgot myself. Following my mother's example, I abandoned my boyself in England.

So rather than dismantle the jam, I idled on the riverbank on the off-chance that a window would appear. Casement, sash, skylight, porthole, leaded, diamond, rose. Water swirled around the roots of old trees, eating away their soil. When will our long affair with the sun end? Twenty-six dead in this tangled dam. Mother's age when I was born, that brief coincidence. Go, go, enough, done.

SUSPENDED SKULL

At the meeting of all who live in the valley to find out what will happen the master pointed the directions. He called the unnamed ancestors.

Zhou Yiyuan and his sister stolid at the edge of the villagers.

The personal is like dew — it forms after midnight and evaporates, on a warm day, before noon. A good story is timeless. Song Wei eclipsed Imogen; her baby is close to being born. All is hard-edged mountain, river lickety-split.

We looked at one another as the elder women warbled their hymns, and families on the wide river spun lazily toward the port. Zhou seemed almost humble, Song distracted.

Our story, yours and mine, when I tell the master, will change everything.

Suspended Lock

Happiness. I love paths that feet have made and felt such joy descending the worn stone steps from the mountain after a climb to see the meadow flowers. While walking I thought about houses and theatres and banks and office buildings — how much of my time used to be spent indoors, looking out of windows — then I wandered through the monastery to the river and along the climbing bank and fell asleep on the red cliff, high above the torrent. *Sun and cloud.* Woke in warm sun, the air claggy with pollen; deer flowed through the bamboo: the shadows of deer: antlers and their echoes. A far-off sneeze. Down at the river, tiny green waves.

Temple Crook

"It will be cosy at home. What about it, buddy-boy? Will we light a fire and get some tea going? Hold your sister's hand." My father said such a thing after a failed meeting with Mum, before we left England, when we were caught in a storm and had to wait a long time for the bus. The three of us miserable and alone, about to leave our world. I missed my father when he died. What I remember most vividly is not what he said, but once in a while feeling him behind me and backing into his legs.

The temperature plunged in the night. Smoke hung in the tops of trees and a veil of rain chilled my skin as we went in to chant the middle of the day.

I'm once again ensconced at West Shrine, waiting for something indistinct, the end of time, the end of our time. Up ahead is the end of my time, round a couple of corners and down that little hill. Perhaps soon. I missed my father and now I miss the old master. Why have I not spoken to Frank? The boats and rafts multiply daily. Has war consumed the rest of the world?

Leading Valley

When the earth began to shake, water spurted from the well and packed dirt lapped the stone sides and ground waves tossed the long boulders into the west plums. Monks and families flew uphill. The storehouse groaned. Above the liquid earth the air was thunderous and thick with cherry blossom. Petals suspended. Earth's weather an ordinary mirage: counterfeit: will all be as it was? How can anything groundless be this beautiful? When I looked, the river was fat, a series of silver crests undulating upstream. On my hand a wound and a moss-green stain. Then part of the mountain fell in a splintering of trees.

Sky Rushing

Before dawn, among secondary tremors, the villagers cleared the ground inside the temple walls of debris and erected a tarp. They carried the bodies of their tribe up and lay them beneath the tarp, beside the dead monks. No one since the ancient battles has witnessed a morning like this. A long eerie silence ended with perpetual traffic teetering along the valley road, military trucks, ambulances, fire engines, buses, flatbeds with equipment, while above our heads helicopters scavenged. River-tumbled bodies. Rocking barges of injured and dying. Aftershocks. Our white-eyed fear.

A day like this is unimaginable until it dawns, brimming with its own reality, the stillest day, the sky crystal blue, warm spring sun on our shoulders. We have broken bones, bruises and cuts. Who did not fall? Still standing are the temple walls, the shrines, the bridge, most of our huts, the bathhouse. A hundred and forty-seven humans, on whose faces grief blooms like a fungus. Our heads down.

FLOATING WHITE

Shock. Aftershock.

YIN PORTALS OF THE HEAD

Memory cannot cope with this agony. From an inconceivable perspective this looks normal, like old documentary footage: *One moment the doctors were crossing the lawn toward the annex, the next they were on their backs, coughing in the thick dust, and the annex was gone.* How simply and quickly we lose speech and only the effort of digging and carrying makes sense. Every muscle aches. We unearth people, one after another, after they are dead. I tweak this one's ear or stroke that one's shaved head, and settle their broken limbs. Living children tumble into my arms. A goat kid stands in a cloud of dust and bleats as if he has been carrying the world on his back and it has almost defeated him.

MASTOID PROCESS

The cave ceremony is underway again, despite the grumbling earth, the same monks who prepared the old master's body prepare the new master's body. A more public funeral continues outside the temple in steady sun amid visiting dignitaries and politicians and impatient journalists.

A woman in a white business suit clutched her microphone, stepped onto the bridge and posed in front of the camera. "The river floods its banks, the monks chant, and behind that broken temple wall — " pointing over her shoulder " — are the bodies of monks and refugees killed in the earthquake . . . "

Root of the Spirit

We are *Suiji.Suiji.* Song Wei's son who drowned. We are now all *Suiji.*

Aftershocks and the sound of timbers groaning in the night woke me over and over from dreams of rubble in smashed bamboo, the faces of the dead, and finally at dawn a perfect tile roof upside down on the ground. At standing prayers a small wind blew centuries of dust and today's yellow pollen gently down from the trees.

It will rain tonight. The well is broken and the river unfit to drink so we carry water from North Spring. Thirty-two dead, eight children, twelve women, twelve men.

We still hold the daily points; I continue, at West Shrine, any time of day or night, to record.

Yang White

The villagers formed a circle in the courtyard around the collapsed well and chanted a prayer in voices I didn't recognise as human.

The dead faces are in the clouds and trees, branches wet from so much rain, eyes immaculate as if catastrophe and deluge have taken turns stirring the pot. Dirty water drips off the bamboo leaves into ruts in the ground, their edges yellow with pollen. Barrel rims also yellow, and crows and old women screaming.

Head Overlooking Tears

A child sat up in her mother's arms and sucked her thumb. Side by side, no longer with us, lay the dead children. The women keened all day and then the village men, too, began to howl. Trees without end on the south hills.

Eye Window

The muscles in my face are rigid. The ground continues to heave. I continue to write, but why? I have never heard or seen anything like this, and it feels as if my nightmares are awake and roaming the valley and I'm close to naming all I have lost. Spring thaw has coincided with the largest quake in centuries, and it is too much. Too much snow, too much rain for the river to handle. When cracks appeared it was too late to run and many died standing up, facing tumbling rocks as big as shrines. And yet I'm left alive, for now, to imagine the river sparkling in summer sun, Imogen stepping off the bridge.

Upright Construction

Time has turned seven hundred years inside out, and manuscripts, ledgers, records, paintings, are gone. Our storehouse is gone. Morning wind tore apart the scarecrow erected by the villagers to guard the temple and flying straw stung our faces.

Let me count my feet, my toes on the ground. It's sunrise. Earth is quiet. Thirty geese arrow west, wavering north then south then north above the bodies of the dead. Sun has returned and the valley is beautiful, new leaves unfurling from plum branches. Blue crow flies through the tallest trees, a hint of black fruit.

I stood earlier among the rows of monks, and the valley seemed a thin place, a narrow place, a single point among countless points. As we filed out of the roofless temple, we began to cry. We heard an answering scream from the forest. Between two roots of a massive curved tree was the crazy elder holding a baby wrapped in silk rags. Without question it was Song's baby, a tiny girl with her mother's features. The old woman murmuring, "She should not be on the ground; she should not be on the earth."

SUPPORT SPIRIT

The young master is dead. Zhou Yiyuan has disappeared. Song Wei is dead and here was her baby in Frank's arms. The old bellringer wore a white robe and had a damaged ankle and had himself to be carried along the path, a monk on either side. A lovely spring day, showers and sun, the five elements in balance. It was a sight to witness, take stock of, the two men conducting the old man cradling the baby girl down the winding path from the ruined temple. When they stopped, I kneeled and touched Frank's feet for not being dead. He rocked the baby, gently shaking his bruised head. The bamboo heavy with rain, the lateral stems hung with silver droplets.

I used to think you loved me. A good review kept me buoyant for days. When things fall into chaos this fast, every twig and root you grasp on your way down snaps clean. And if nights are a bounty of failure, days are hopeful because of scudding clouds, hours of sun and singing birds.

The work now contemplates us as we stack the salvaged items, burn the damaged and useless, shift the manageable rocks and stones from the grounds. The first laugh from the village relieved everything, and *lift* was tangible when the night bell was struck. I experienced it with you once or twice, this lift. Laughter has thrown a bridge to the recently dead, and the result is a quick strand between sky and earth, almost invisible, drifting in wind that has freshness in it.

Supplies arrive tomorrow. Chainsaws wail in the rubble. This afternoon ministers and prefects crossed the river to assess the damage and to be photographed with monks and wreckage. Deputations of builders have been dispatched from cities across the plain. This morning five boys, their heads already shaved, showed up at North Gate. Five more stepped off crowded barges an hour ago.

Brain Hollow

Morning birds were singing and I was thinking coffee, coffee and a cigarette, maybe a shot of whisky. Past the broken well and the fallen storehouse to the temple to the minor west shrine. Through half-closed lids, I saw in the distance the stranger, the spy, the father, alone under the warrior tree. He sat quietly and a small girl, one of the new orphans, darted through the outer gate and clambered into his lap, and I knew he had lost everything.

It is not easy to count to thirty-two. It took me the rest of the day. At dusk a twig fell from a stone. Rather: a signal caught my eye: a shift in the fabric, that twinkle again. Thirty-two birds had gone to roost; now only one held forth, a song for each of our fallen, for each of our dead. The girl in the man's arms was knocking on his head; when he looked at her and let her go, she climbed into the warrior tree, into the branches above him; it was too dark to make out anything else.

It was always important, was it not, to imagine carefully, get a sense of how we all fit together, actors, audience, stage manager, lighting designer, director, writer? Thirty-two is sixty-four parents and one hundred and twenty-eight grandparents.

Wind Pool

Above the temple North Spring still flows as clear as ever (Spring at the Crook, Liver-8, *He*-Sea and water point). We all gathered this morning to hold Wind Pool and Spring at the Crook, wood yin and yang, before we began to collect our water for the day. From Frank's mound (Gall Bladder-34, Yang Mound Spring, a heavenly star point) the extent of the ruins is a new surprise.

A blue wave sloshed in my bucket as I trudged the temple path (they were building straw beds in the temple and preparing fires) to the storehouse courtyard, past the guests and through the gates, and down to the bridge to cleanse the river. I set down the bucket and made a wish. The wave spiralled briefly green into the brown turbulence. There were vultures in the grey sky and wounds on the inside of my fingers. When I lifted my head smoke was filtering through the bamboo to join towering grey clouds.

Shoulder Well

"We must nourish blood and yin."

I and three others carried bucket after bucket from the spring down to where the old women were cooking rice for visitors, monks and villagers. At the cave the death monks were chanting. We gathered, the monks from this and other monasteries and the people from villages in the region, the abbots and politicians from capital cities, at the edge of the forest.

"Will you leave?" Frank asked.

"I can't leave now."

"I might leave."

"And go where?"

"How is the question."

"You can't go."

"Not yet. But I forget what I was doing here. It's fading. I forgot to bless those I could have blessed. Who do you wish you had blessed?"

At the cave they were chanting. Frank and I turned in that direction and, just like my lonesome and foolish father, as unready as him, I thought of obligation and obedience.

"My son," I said. "My parents and sister, Song Wei, her baby, Zhou Yiyuan. You, Frank. The old master, the young master. Imogen."

"Maybe I'll go with the homeless," he said.

MAY

HOLD THE BABY AND HER FACE TILTS AS though she sees something above, her mouth opens — something to say? — starhands float from her body, and she grows heavy. I look down into her blue eyes and lose where I am in favour of someplace I've never been, though it is familiar. Here's a split, a fracture, now the valley has cracked open, but my heart can't squeeze out of my chest since there's no wound, not yet. I'm falling and want to soar.

Rain began to tick on the ground. Outside the shrine the old woman smiled up, *Give me the child*, and made rocking motions with her cradling arms and I passed her the baby.

"I had a thought." Frank squatted with his legs apart, bony knees pointing opposite directions. He stroked his bandaged ankle. "You need not write anymore."

The rift is in me now, like the horizon, part of the world I've always known but never recognised for what it really was. I have swallowed the split the way the valley has swallowed and quietly digested its own revelations. Touch my own chest — ticker, muscle, fist — read its language. Unbelievable, anyway.

"I didn't feel this presence at all when holding my own son," I told Frank. "Have I forgotten?"

My own son. Such an old memory of night swimming, a piece of jetsam butting rhythmically against the least physical part of me — my body turning into a swarm of fishes, a school of birds, a storm of flies, a murder of splinters, and coming apart, the human world too full and likewise coming apart, and the long trip westward nearly done, all but.

Armpit Abyss

"I cannot tell you what to do," Frank said.

"I can't stop."

"Chaos and order." His eyes twinkled in the firelight. The rain had paused and the old woman had taken away the baby. "If what you meet tells its name, say hello. If there's an answer, you will hear your own name."

My feet were dusty. I sat on the edge of the shrine and smiled at my toes. A bird rattled in the bamboo, settling. There was a gap called Change in the ligament between her body and her wing. There was an earthworm cast by my instep.

If the invisible worm changes the earth, this tells us something of our little travels. If I and the worm share the same physical dimension and thought-space, then traffic stands still and all journeys come under review. What have we learned while eating and shitting and walking to and fro? Only that everything can be copied. That the recorded evidence of everything multiplies every nanosecond. That accumulation takes all our time. Time, needless to say, is smaller than it used to be. Now is ridiculous. And heart-shaped. Of the things I have met recently, stars and earthworms left a trace.

Flank Sinews

I walked uphill and stopped. Nothing was missing. Wait. Listen. No, nothing was missing. In my nostrils the smell of cut grass. Then nothing. Then an orange balloon trailing a short string crossed the sky west, gaining altitude as it vanished, and I knew a string was in my fingers once. When I wasn't afraid of losing things. The cat on the back of my legs as I lay on my belly and read when I was nine or eight and truly dreaming: the cat, the book, the carpet, electric fire, diamond window. Scripts, actors and lines.

"Still at it?" said Frank, and he limped into the shrine and sat: "The old master once told me to focus only on small things and animals and people. *Stay calm: the smallest things are beautiful.* But they wear out."

Back to the page, ravaged by completion. Too much body. What to do? The massive abstractions and universalities and anonymous figures arrive anyway, propelled down institutional corridors by their own momentum, lodging in the pericardium, a *tick* to the heart's *tock. Stay calm.*

The afternoon was tranquil. Spring an interval lit by quiet light. Imogen will walk across the bridge, through all this rubble, and life will be unbroken again.

Illness at bay. Pain at bay. False endings left on the cutting room floor. False paternities baying at the moon. Morphine. My father after surgery, smiling at my mother. The end of history is the beginning of.

Sun and Moon

For years I drove under dark clouds to and from work, the work of moving parts forward and holding others back, shoving traits together then breaking them apart, sweeping up fallen fragments after the rehearsal, joining the sheered bits to other characteristics for later roles; for future selves to sift through in shifts — one set of tired eyes replaced by another. Meanwhile making hay while the sun shines, meeting the agent over lunch, signing a contract in the afternoon. Trips to the drug store for amphetamines, quick drink at the restaurant bar down the alley from the guitar shop, home to late news, night-night to the boy. Who was it detected wisdom in Hamlet's madness? Pause on the upstairs landing, in terror at failing memory — Alzheimer's, amnesia, brain tumour, aphasia. Ah — Claudius?

CAPITAL GATE

And so, try to comprehend the whole by snagging a piece and spending one lifetime in its investigation. This leaf, new green, and its sister seedpod touched with red, in a blue sky, leaf and pod backlit by the west sun. But at the bottom of the cliff behind the cave is the complete skeleton of a deer spread out over several feet, the skull below the ribs, sacrum above the skull, leg bones splayed like spokes of a wheel — a throw to forecast the valley's fate after this quake. Find a deer, put the seedpod on the sacrum, make a wish. Since I was a boy I have been marking time, measuring my passage, waiting for a girl.

GIRDLING VESSEL

Found the deer. Found the seedpod. With a glance up at treetops and bamboo against fresh snow on the mountains, smoke pluming from funeral fires, I set the pod on the bone.

Deities have flocked in: TV crews and students with tiny sound recorders sneak around monks turning prayer wheels, villagers and carpenters doggedly at their business. But this is not the film industry. This is not a thesis or a smart investment. There has been violence in the valley and this is my record. Here's the story I want: at the end of things, boy and man ride forward together, speaking easily to each other, while animals gather, curious about their fleeting scent.

FIVE PIVOTS

I took my son camping, just the two of us, and we spent the day watching eagles drift in front of our noses at the edge of the cliff. Far below were ducks on the small bay, and in the distance the mountain range of an American peninsula. The day on the cliff edge with my son was the day of days. That light was the light of light.

Spring is always heavy. Real nests are already occupied by fledglings, whose tweets I'd recognise anywhere. I made my penis hard and was amazed that after such a long time I produced so little. The quake turned the world inside out and its effects were catastrophic, yet when I turned myself inside out the yield was paltry. My heart clanked and the valley's music returned amplified.

The bell, knocked sideways, has been reframed. Some heard it clang at the time of the shock. I heard only splintering wood and the groaning of bedrock.

My mother came home from visiting dad in the hospital and said she was done, and recognised nothing, and that was that, except for the bitterness. Dad died a year later.

Linking Path

The days quicken. Technology, the fence around the institution, whose utility is too confused to answer the simplest question (as if an institution can do other than infinitely complicate a question), thrums the air even here. The quake was bigger, though. Our invented forms can't keep up with life and death.

I squatted to shit and looked into a wall of green — life so varied that the measurers and modellers and physicists are millennia at their desks — and wondered if it wasn't all just projection and coincidence. These confabulations. The songbirds might be fewer, but the unfolding of wings is still beyond our comprehension.

Stationary Crevice

Nothing. Hold Gall Bladder-29 in the hip between superior iliac spine and greater trocanter. Then the path opens west, following the sun, the way life continues if you give still intervals between windy thoughts a little attention. Between no and thing is a breathing space and something else — the end of control, the willing time where a seed sticks and calls for moisture. Before the *no* is the complete story of light, no death near it. In the end a tree splits the hipbone and leaves cover the ground, the last shrivelled fruit softens and falls. There is the mud splash. There is frog-light, the earth covered with pale green bodies. There is water-light, shadows rippling over the trees near the bank. There is land-light, soft and reluctant. There's light in the vivid green sky and clouds bigger than hurricanes closing fast from the east. Children pause in their game to look up. Straight-edged rain divides the hissing river from the hissing trees. When we close our eyes light stays, and in America and Canada we know our

children are safe by the electric zap of bug killers in neighbour-
hoods filled with accountants.

Jumping Circle

A morning of complete harmony. Sun sat close with each blade of
new grass down to the river. Beyond the courtyard, forests tipped
the blue. We kneeled in a circle to share food, the village elders and
the monks and some government members, to consider the future.

"This monastery has retained its hiddenness, its secrecy," said
an official dressed in blue fatigues. "It is still a lost monastery."

"We know this," said Frank.

Carefully, I picked the blades of grass that threatened the
stepping-stones.

"A mushroom ring has appeared in the soil outside the cave,"
said one of the new monks.

"Why not?" said Frank.

"Help will come the way it has always come," said the
governor, "from the river."

The elder women nodded. The crazy one who minded Song
Wei's baby said, "And on the next fire night the river will stop
flowing and something new will step out."

"Thank you," said Frank.

"What is her name?" I asked the crazy one. "What is the
baby's name?"

A politician read from a document and placed a cheque on
the ground in the middle of the circle. The breeze promptly took
the paper and the politician gave a little cry. His associate reacted
quickly and snapped the cheque from the air. Everyone laughed.

Wind Market

Once I had a birthday cake, chocolate, with candles, all blue. Each slice had a candle. I held my breath. Eight, nine, ten. This was the year my parents emigrated and I lost my accent and my tongue got tied and the shapes of words were wrong in my mouth.

Middle Ditch

There is the walled garden, not to be entered. No sign of Zhou Yiyuan.

Knee Yang Gate

Frank is the new master. He sat on the seat outside the garden's tall door in morning sunshine. Earth-moving machinery beeped: backing up. The wall coping made wave shadows, a fringe on the worn timbers.

"I thought you were leaving."

He raised his head. "I thought you were staying?"

"I am staying."

"That's news to me."

Yang Mound Spring

The crazy village woman boiled tea and we sat across from each other in silence. "Where is the baby," I asked.

She grinned and thumbed to the next hut where the woman I had treated in the winter was stirring a pot. The baby's head covered her breast.

Each bell today reminded me of Yang Mound Spring, Frank's hut and the point in the tender depression below and outside the knee.

Losing an accent is not like losing a language: it is a voluntary betrayal of identity, a sacrifice of ancestral music, a refusal to risk being misunderstood.

Yang Intersection

Frank and I walked north along the garden's east wall, listening to the two monks inside shovelling, scraping, chopping. Left up the steep rock along the north wall, left along the dark west wall, left, the south wall, and back to the door.

"How has the quake affected what is inside?" I asked.

"The gardeners sound busy," said Frank.

"I've imagined my parents inside, or Zhou Yiyuan concocting a brand new universe."

"Have you?"

Outer Hill

Behind the wall was the noise of water running, perhaps a waterfall, and then a splash, as of a great fish leaping from the surface of a pond. The crunch of slow receding footsteps. A hummingbird twanged at my ear.

Directly below, through the bamboo forest, was the stretch of deep river where the two children fell and Suiji drowned. Swallows hunted the surface.

"How is the rest of the world faring?" said Frank. "The doctors? Their dewy lawn? Imogen?"

Bright Light

The garden introduces at least the notion of garden. Water flows, and since no water enters or leaves, the garden must contain its own weather, rivers and seas.

Suppose the walls enclose a forest, ancient and thousands of meters high, the trees so closely packed that only a child can enter (I'm too big, too old) and standing by the open garden door are my parents, powerful demigods on holiday from their busy negotiations of immigration and shooting schedules and hospitals and ferries and pathology reports, and the gist of their wordless message is *wait*.

When I told Frank, he said, "That's optimistic."

"The quake, surely, was an aspect of a wider cataclysm. Just as the garden is the region in microcosm, this valley must be a kind of universal gazetteer."

"Is that what you believe?"

"Can I go in?"

"Possibly."

"When?"

"I guess we could climb the wall."

"Don't you have the key?"

"Zhou Yiyuan has the key."

"Why? You've seen him?"

"Not yet. I'm looking for signs of Zhou Yiyuan."

A goat approached, her new kid alongside.

Yang Assistance

The gardeners enter the garden, then there's the sound of scraping. Asleep on my feet, bladder points all sore, I spent the afternoon digging a ditch above New East Shrine.

Suspended Bell

Night rehearsal of the absence of children.

Hill Ruins

Sudden and brief torrents of rain. Ribbons of sun last thing before night. I tried to remember being a boy, a son. What did I do with my father? Cricket? Football? There: a rectangle of field beside the school; there: my dad's voice, "Not like that. Not like that."

Foot Overlooking Tears

The past has receded leaving only worm casts, broken branches, debris, seed husks. Enough to build a life, perhaps. No matter. Life included joy. Now its erotic promise is enshrined in Imogen's pending visit; one more season to see through, then summer and her arrival.

Earth Five Meetings

"I dreamed I flew home," I said, "and home looked exactly like this — same birds, trees, clouds, same people."

Frank chuckled. "Was I there?"

"I don't think so."

"Good."

In the paddies the grains were plump. I held his hand as we circled the garden wall, ears pricked for any sound; then I left him on the bench by the door and descended alone by a remote path to the bridge then uphill to the temple.

I will find Zhou Yiyuan, get the key and take Imogen into the garden this summer, no matter what it takes — what a child I am! — and we will stage a wedding scene; but which scene, what play?

PINCHED RAVINE

Days have a shape. This day began slowly and was supposed to go *slow, quick, slow/quick, slow*, these time signatures pencilled across an indeterminate number of dimensions. Then, as morning got underway the first *slow* got quick too fast and the first *quick* vanished, then the second *quick* seemed endless cacophony, and then it collided with the last *slow*. Afternoon was a long unexpected dwindling and now, under the influence of a brief and gorgeous sunset, signalled by bird flight and the memory of Active Pass and snow on a girl's shoulders, I anticipate the briefest *quick* and a slow evening.

YIN PORTALS OF THE FOOT

The first roses were open in the hedgerow along the road. The bridge to my young great grandparents in England, surely. Tapping sounds from the walled garden. The path to the river was loud: a monk with a chainsaw was bucking up a tree felled by the earthquake, sawdust streaming in early morning light. The scent of sap mixed with the memory of roses. Smell of roses.

Large Hill   Yin Wood

"I don't know about living in a monastery," I said.

Frank's face looked soft, his lips curving. We were about to descend from the garden door to the river.

"None of this is mine, none of it."

The familiar smile creased his face. "Am I here?"

"Yes, Frank, you are still here."

Voices below caught his attention. "What is that?"

"There are people on the bridge," I said.

He turned his head as if looking down to the river. "Are they leaving or arriving?"

"I don't know."

"What would you guess?"

"It looks like a meeting."

"I wouldn't be surprised. Is Zhou Yiyuan among them?"

I stared at the tiny figures on the bridge. "I can't tell. I don't think so."

He held up his hand and there was dirt on his wrist, his fingers. "It's not your business anymore, but I'm expecting him."

"What have you heard?"

"I have heard that your master—" He paused. "It's always like this in spring," he said. "The river brown and full of debris, people coming and going, monks asking idiotic questions."

Moving Between

"I'm tired of my own voice," I said.

"Stop speaking," Frank said.

He stood at my side in silence. The bell sounded and a fish rose from the deep shadow beneath the bridge, the carp's sleek body working the current. High above the snowline three birds turned lazy arcs. Nothing today was rushed.

GREAT RUSHING

"How is your apprentice doing?"

"Late, early, muffled."

"You should fire him."

"Perhaps I will."

"Every second person's stumbling along with a crutch, arm in a sling, there are suits everywhere, and have you heard the howls at night?"

"We have had an earthquake. I thought you were tired of speaking."

"I am."

We sat in the warm shrine.

"I'm writing with a pencil."

"Where's your pen?" he asked.

"Lost."

"Brush?"

"Lost."

"Mine too."

MIDDLE SEAL

Sun on black bamboo. The sky silver inside, outside brass. I kneeled on the bank to wash a grazed knuckle and the river carried away my blood.

The willows leaned over the water, tendrils in relief against an inverted silver plate. Gulls dipping wings.

Woodworm Ditch

"I'm tired of my words."

"Stop writing," he said.

"All words. All signs."

"Where are they directing you?"

We were in our shrine and a storm was approaching, trees hissing again at the edge of the forest. He washed his hands and dried them carefully before taking up a small bag. He produced two brushes and gave me one.

"I have decided to map the old grounds while the memory of its shape is fresh."

"It hasn't changed much," I said.

"You are blind."

The wind gathered force and shook the trees. He hunkered down to draw the mountain and river, using a grey wash for terraces and forests and stands of bamboo, an inkier wash for the village. Slow work for him, the temple, storehouse, shrines, huts, bathhouse, trees, paths, wind buffeting his bent back. After an hour he lifted his head and smiled. "Why did we not make maps before?"

And I remembered it was Ophelia's father, yes, Claudius' advisor, yes. But it wasn't wisdom that Polonius found in Hamlet's madness, it was method. Ah, yes. Method. Plan.

Frank set aside the large paper to dry, and I helped him anchor it to the boards with four stones. He stood and stretched and fumbled for his stick.

I'm slow to make English words with a brush, but the labour gives me great pleasure. Who would follow a blind man's map? Frank is the master I have been waiting for. Sun glints on the crude map he has made and it seems the work of a clumsy child. When I think this something squirms inside my belly. When I'm done, I stretch my hands high in the air.

Central Capital

At dawn the monastery grounds lay in a slight mist, green and gentle, beautifully tranquil. Frank led a party of us through the bamboo forest, following the zigzag path to the edge of the wild land.

Later, I found a letter addressed to the old master and postmarked Los Angeles in the company trailer near the bridge. I carried it through the courtyard, past the storehouse construction zone, up to Frank's hut.

We sat on the bench beside the window and he opened the envelope and felt the texture of the paper. As he stroked the words with a finger the bell sounded and he paused while the deep peals blew round us.

"I did not fire him," he said.

"No."

"I hope this boy will learn to invite the bell. He is very bad." He replaced the paper in the envelope. "Tell me what you expect."

"Nothing."

He held the letter in the air. "Read it to me."

Knee Joint

I'm not afraid of losing track since I lost track long ago, left matters behind, all but this body and mental bits caught in transit, which I keep in a small valise in a corner of my hippocampus: the shopping lists and scout records and posters and programs and licences and passports. Undeniably mine, just less significant than the Italian hilltop church whose steps I once climbed. They come from my sixty-eight years. Broke another tooth last week. The letter from Imogen was imprecise as to her plans. I keep checking the bridge, afraid I might miss her arrival.

This morning the deck was silver in the low east light and there were footsteps in the dew, two sets, one leading south, the other north. Someone had left and returned or someone had come and gone away again. Other possibilities existed but they were meaningless.

Every day we work together, Frank on his maps, I on these words. Can't help ourselves. We walk side by side in silence around the garden wall. We meditate. We listen critically to the apprentice ringing the bell.

"He is getting worse, not better," he murmurs.

"Have you seen Zhou Yiyuan?"

"He is alive."

"Are you leaving?"

"Are you?"

"Not before she comes."

"And then?"

"Not only am I afraid of going away, I'm afraid of anything new."

"How are you at bell ringing?"

"No sense of rhythm."

"Gardening?"

"Did you get the key?"

"I told the television people not to film inside the grounds."

Thirty-two deaths have transformed this place. Overseers and government agents and ministers are a weekly occurrence. Battle fronts have been reconfigured and nights are quiet. This afternoon the TV crew built a track along the south bank of the river and ran their camera back and forth, its long lens like a machine gun, while men and women with phones stumbled up and down our paths, all vanishing into the forest at the director's command.

Spring at the Crook

The crew have retreated for now, but the grasses by the river have been trampled flat. I'm looking for that word again, the word to describe the kind of writing that concerns a journey divided into episodes, increasingly outrageous, the rhythm creating a mounting intensity. I catch it then it's gone. A Japanese word? *Haibun?* No. Spanish, of Moorish derivation, the journey through a desert, Spanish or North African. A dusty lane through flat brown country, days of boredom between vivid encounters. Closer. Don Quixote riding the latest model through ranks of giant metal windmills shrieking and whirling under the stark sun. All the locals thin and savage. Give it up. No, what is it? Serial going, with flair . . . Before we spread east and west, didn't we surge north, a small band of us, from Africa, and what did we call that? The word, should I remember it, would tie *where we came from* to *why we are here.* Would listing our sympoms jog memory? Buying and selling, keeping accounts, pulling up stakes. Sleep, work, eat, spend, migrate. I can't remember cash in the pocket and haven't received payment for services, haven't paid a single bill, and haven't bought anything, not even a book, for a long time. All gone, the things acquired sold, the money given away, the last spent on travel. Acquisition is the perfect betrayal of childhood. Acquisition of money, the adult symptom, distinguishes adult from child, separates the trader from the hunter.

The cure is a deep settling.

Do the garden walls contain Africa? A swatch of Europe, tribal wars and Ethnic conflagration? Atlantic? Pacific?

Relax. Easy. I think it begins with *p*.

Frank lets out a long sigh and lifts his head from his latest map as if searching the sky. It's almost evening and darkness, texture ahead of the thing itself, has slipped in from the east. He bends to add a quick line between his thumb and forefinger planted on the paper.

JUNE

Yin Envelope

ACROSS THE LAWN THEY COME, THE DOCTORS, in a small group, laughing and talking together and, amazing thing, the central figure, a tall man in a white shirt with an open collar, stops, and a tear rolls down his left cheek, then a second. He holds up his hands to mask his face. There is a word to describe this kind of waiting, but I can't remember it, only the shape, like the double curve a child draws to suggest a bird in flight. The other word, the writing-journey word, is more alive, closer but still elusive. The doctor's hands meet in prayer, in front of his throat.

Our son walked past the flowering trees in Amsterdam, his shoulders squared in the steady rain, his figure getting smaller and smaller, the street impressionist greys and greens and pinks.

Leg Five Miles

I remember going to the store to buy milk early in the morning, crows calling across the alley, spring sun after a long winter, my bike gliding around potholes, cat on a sunny fence. That word, that word. It is French or Spanish. The journey broken up, the hero a fool with barely enough wit to be a rogue.

The doctors make trails in the dewy grass. They are like children on a free day walking to the river, all but the tall serious man, their bodies too jazzed not to play. It begins almost certainly with *p*, the journey-word, and perhaps the waiting word begins with *r*.

Frank has suggested we go swimming together. He's afraid he will be swept away and lost, that he will vanish without a trace if he goes alone. He used to be a strong swimmer, he said. He learned to swim in America, before he was blind, and once swam with Thomas Cleary in Lake Michigan. He and the old master always went swimming in the river, every spring to fall, even last summer, though the old master had difficulty climbing in and out. But this year, after all that has happened, Frank is weak and lame, and must swim with someone sound, someone he trusts.

YIN CORNER

A noun and adjective, but maybe just an adjective. Weather slanting in with the light, until clouds shut half the sky, three quarters — a lid loose at the edges, imperfect fit. The head doctor has returned to his family again, his intrepid, optimistic colleagues, and all of them are pleased to see him. *Why sad? Why the long face?* Pacing the green room, the wings: remember, remember.

URGENT PULSE

The doctors crossing the lawn, laughing, all but the chief waving their arms and swivelling their heads as they get closer. A knot of cheerful women and men, rank and discipline forgotten. The chief bows his head and places his hands palm to palm. A chittering in the hedgerow, flight and a settling flourish: a robin sits her nest, a real bird, real nest, actual eggs, everything to lose. As the doctors close in, a new thought comes — so right that my knees go weak and a shiver threatens to unhinge my bones.

The world is the red crown of my dad's head, these clouds his thin white hair, and my mother's blue eyes are the sky.

The doctors approach across the lawn. The chief about to retire; on this last day at the hospital, he will consider his last case, his last intervention.

"It is many years since I watched a movie," said Frank. "Tell me where I have seen you."

A breathtaking spring breeze blew through the writing shrine as I took my brush to today's entry.

CAMPHORWOOD GATE

God is a vine rose climbing where the fallen fell, where the storehouse fell, blooming on its highest branches only, roots in the swamp. And all between roots and flowers is a thorny tangle: tree: birds, sweet air.

Down by the river the villagers are busy with their next migration.

A black-and-white photograph tucked in the corner of my dressing room mirror. Doctors on a sanatorium lawn, relaxing before the official pose.

CYCLE GATE

The storehouse rebuilding has begun in earnest. Artisans from another sect use a corner of the temple as their field office. They are quiet men, surly even. I do not quite trust them. They are more friendly with the remaining villagers than with their fellow monks. They seem to resent something — being here, this work, the place itself.

Today we dug clay for a wall to prevent the ramshackle town from being swept away by the rising river even though the families will soon move on. Frank suggested the village be moved to higher ground. The water level this morning was four metres higher than yesterday. And to think we were swimming just a few days ago. I cannot comprehend anything. I was just talking to my wife on a park bench. We were keeping tabs on our son paddling in a little pond. Remember the Kitsilano park between the ocean and the city, a tunnel of shade in the hottest months, remnant stream meandering through long sticky grass? She asked me what was in store for us, and I touched her hand. Then I was not acting, not a husband, but something far more intimate and mysterious. A crow was washing itself in the green water. Our son saw us and turned heel and ran up the hill to the swing set. An indelible moment of discovery and guilt.

All manner of items are rushing through the valley on the surging flood: whole trees, bamboo walls, a leopard, a herd of deer, sections of roofs, and a small intact mountain shrine, very old, its carvings scrubbed clean.

◯

Meeting of Yin   Conception

Soon the doctors will cease their diagnostic confabulations, resume their playful antics and continue forward, like advancing troops, across the open lawn.

A child is hiding at the edge of the forest — I saw her a moment ago, the flash of red, a pale hand. A breeze spins the leaves of the old trees in front of the shrine. The rape. The hospital. The storehouse. There is no storehouse. No hospital.

CURVED BONE

And what if Imogen never comes and I never leave and wars escalate? Suppose life simply dwindles to an end. Suppose life ends, *click*. What is the equation for time and space excluding life? The three or four trillion suns that lit the dusty path one evening when I was quite young. Bits of world rushing through the gorge. Storm tears wet my face. Stomach trouble. Granddad said when you're old, pains attack and vanish, take no notice; then he died. Dad went to colon cancer and Mother went to suicide. Way way go away. Go go go away. The child at the treeline, a little way into the forest, waiting to be found. Way way go away. Go go go away. Nothing further to report? Nothing to record. A little boredom. Plugged sinuses. A stomach ache. A Mahler melody stuck in the head.

MIDDLE POLE

The warrior tree has been encircled and healed. The new well is blessed. All these words are guesses and wishes. I worked on one of the village women. During the quake she'd fallen and cracked some vertebrae. Her body released its pain, channel by channel, till she was asleep, and I stood at her side and smoothed the air above her, head to toes, our bellies in tune. Something invisible thickened above the horizon of her old breasts and lean hips and thighs.

ORIGIN PASS

On the path a dead rat. Hail in the morning, sun in the afternoon. I love this more than I can say. What is the equation for life? All the movies, all the paintings, all the novels. All the directors I ever worked with. All music.

STONE GATE

Every walk home through the rain. The river. Textbooks. Good friends. Shakespeare. Words. A blast of hail on the roof late in the day. The village woman saying thanks. Frank certain of his way downhill. Pouring rain. The deer bones. My heavy head in my hands.

SEA OF QI

Both parents alive, smiling across the table — nothing yet of the undignified illnesses to come, the cycles of resistance and resignation. Julian of Norwich accepting a nice cup of tea from Archbishop Arundel. "Oneing" and "noughting." *All shall be*

well and all shall be well, and all manner of thing shall be well.
Ah me Mum and Dad, all at sea with googling and blogging,
unfriending and friending. *Shewing of Love.* The baby's pursed
lips. My pursed lips. "Bowl of rice, milk?"

"What is the point?" Frank asked.

"Sea of *Qi.*"

"What is the vessel?"

"*Ren mo*, Conception, Central Channel."

"Please find this point on my body."

He lay on his back and I kneeled beside him. The corner of
his latest map was soaked with rain, the ink blurring. I placed
my left middle finger, Pericardium-9, Middle Rushing, just
below his belly button.

"What is there?"

"The Great."

"What is the *qi*?"

"Subtle."

"What do you find in this point?"

"Binary fission. A going and a coming."

"Yes?"

"So different from what I expected."

"Yes?"

"A baby girl."

"Is she yin?"

"Yin of yin."

"Good. This is the Cinnabar Field. Please find and hold
Mingmen, Gate of Life . . . ah . . . " He deflated between my
hands. "Tomorrow you will leave the valley," he said. "You will
smell the outside world. It's arranged."

Doctors surrounded me, discussing my past, my symptoms.
Once upon a time. Sweetheart. Do you see what is happening?

"Do you hear me?" he said.

"I'm not ready."

Beyond Frank's settled body I could see the warrior tree. I felt the bell's reverberations in my bones. Young crows cackled and screeched in the forest. Sun slanted through the west boundary plums.

"These days," he said, "we must do things we do not want to do. I did not want to be master."

"Where will I go?"

"As with any journey, you will travel." His frail thready pulse thrummed between my fingers. "The villagers have rescued an eagle with a broken wing on the mountain; now they must care for it. Zhou Yiyuan has returned, and you are leaving, which you did not choose."

Yin Intersection

At the bridge the three of us bowed and Zhou Yiyuan held out his hand. I stepped back onto Frank's foot and he yelled and cracked his stick against the rail.

"What is happening?" I asked. "Are we all going?"

But no one answered, no one spoke, and we set off. Zhou Yiyuan led us across the bridge to the road and a brand new blue Toyota truck.

The gas and brake pedals had been fitted with extensions so Zhou could reach. He perched on his cushion and drove all morning, peering over the dash, his big shoulders hunched, through villages and towns and stretches of rough hilly country, then stopped at a small city where we bought gas and shopped for food. Once we were provisioned he sped the three of us along a busy street and parked the truck outside a café.

We sat through the afternoon in the tiny dim place. Zhou said he had satellite phone, GPS unit, water filtration system, all arranged. We would paddle to a remote island, to a prehistoric site. Sparks flew between him and Frank as they sipped green tea, then rice wine. Outside the window the rainy street swarmed with bicycles and motorcycles and pedestrians; loaded troop-carriers rumbled by.

Back in the truck we drove north all night.

"Something gathers to gather us," said Zhou Yiyuan, slapping the steering wheel.

"I told you not to say wise stupid things," said Frank.

They were pleased with themselves and couldn't stop grinning and cracking jokes.

SPIRIT GATE

We travelled most of the next day and night, slept a few hours at a small inn on the coast and in the morning picked up two kayaks, a yellow double and a red single, and drove northeast to a fishing village on a deep inlet and by midafternoon were standing in the vanguard of a storm on a headland beside a research centre. Overhead, flags flapped and dark clouds passed south. Spits of rain in our faces. Salt stinging our eyes. Wind flicked the tops of waves. A lonesome, frightening, daunting place and yet our ease with one another was all at once wide, wide as childhood. Frank had paddled a kayak on Lake Michigan; Zhou Yiyuan was familiar with these waters. There, in the research centre parking lot, we unloaded the truck, stuffed food and clothes into waterproof bags.

WATER DIVIDE

We lashed the kayaks to an aluminium frame welded to the deck of the old fishboat, and stowed our gear in a heap behind the wheelhouse. Then the boat bounced through the inlet toward a string of grey islands.

"What are those birds?" I asked.

"Sea swallows," shouted Zhou Yiyuan.

"He means storm petrels," said Frank.

After an hour, the boat nosed onto a gravel bar at the end of the peninsula, and we jumped off and Zhou and I unloaded kayaks, tent, sleeping bags and mats, food and whisky, and watched the boat power away.

Frank sat on the gravel facing the ocean.

Silence. No wind. Pebbles scattered underfoot. Rotting seaweed. With Scotch in plastic glasses, we toasted our lives.

"What I want to know," I said, "is what are we looking for? What are we doing?"

No one answered.

We packed all the stuff into the kayaks and climbed into our cockpits. I'd done this before. Long ago in another life, but it was strange to be sitting in the ocean again. Snug. Alone. Not alone. Zhou's access to equipment and technology, the master's presence, their clowning, our unspoken mission — no need to know. This was a great relief.

We paddled out into the running sea, Frank in the cockpit ahead of me, his back straight, his red life jacket too tight, his arms flailing, Zhou solo in the red boat to our right.

On the first island we reached was a beach looking southeast into open water. We pitched our tent. The sun set across the palm trees and the continent behind.

LOWER CAVITY

Slept late. Breakfast and a slow packing up. At noon, we carried the kayaks from the high-tide line to the water's edge. Paddled north across a choppy strait, surfing a following sea, far apart, yet keeping each other in sight. From inside a trough, I could see nothing but water and sky, the occasional smear of Zhou Yiyuan's red boat. We landed on a wide bay on another island. The white sandy beach was scattered with perfectly round stones. Bear prints led into the forest and Zhou and I left the master to rest and followed the tracks to a sunlit lake. Exquisitely still, as if everything was asleep. Under the surface fallen trees. Weed covered a third of the water.

That evening we paddled to the next island — hours of working against a rising wind — arriving stiff, weary, with barely enough light to haul the boats above the high tide line. Secured them bow-to-bow to a wind-sculpted tree. Made camp and ate in the dark. Built a fire and settled down to drink whisky, exhausted, long into the night.

STRENGTHEN THE INTERIOR

"Look, stars," I said.
    "Not stars," said Zhou, "phosphorescence."
    "Some of it is reflected stars."
    "Ask Frank."
    The light in the water.
    "Tell him what we came for," said Zhou.
    "The caves. To offer a bowl of rice."
    By noon we were paddling a minor sea surrounded by islands. Fish-eye lens. We struggled up a tidal river into a lagoon on a large island. Deck-mounted camera. Helicopter shot. Handheld. Portaged to another lagoon: three connected lakes, less and less salty.

    On the last lake, we rested our paddles and drifted beneath the overgrown ruins of a temple, gibbons howling from the crumbling walls. We floated on the drowsy lake, almost asleep among chorusing birds and insects and monkeys. Trees festooned with vines and lichen. Hothouse. Steam room. Flies and mosquitoes hovered in the intense heat of the afternoon and dragonflies dipped wings on the mirror surface.

MIDDLE CAVITY

That evening, at the northeast end of the island, Zhou and I looked for the caves, but found only black volcanic rock pools full of anemones and starfish and crabs. And one well-inflated basketball. We bounced it off sheets of rock. Swam in the deepest pool.

We ate around the fire, drinking whisky.

"Your directions were wrong," Zhou Yiyuan said. "This is the wrong island."

"No," said Frank.

"You are blind."

"A natural deviation."

"What will happen to a monastery run by a blind monk?"

"New channels are opening," Frank said. "New paths, new points, new flows."

"How can new paths show up?" I asked.

"Through meditation," said Frank. "Through crisis. Ancestral intervention."

"Do the points ever change?" I said. "Are new points found?"

"No. Perhaps. Not by us."

The ocean, silent at his back, caught light in its ripples; a distant beacon winked.

Zhou rocked on his heels, staring at the master. "And you don't miss women?"

Upper Cavity

I woke before Zhou Yiyuan and Frank and clambered north along the shore; paused in a small bay, amid the jagged igneous rock and tide pools: high in the surrounding cliffs birds were swooping out of three openings.

A tight chimney climb — fissure with toe-holds — to a flat hallway carpeted with wildflowers, crushed and broken shells. Nothing but the bay and the ocean and the wide calm faded eastern horizon. Sun shone into each cave, directly onto sea swallows sitting eggs beneath grotesque figures etched into the stone walls.

When I returned we ate an enormous breakfast and drank the last whisky. Zhou and I played basketball on the hard sand, open ocean rolling in, wind-black. He lobbed a high looping ball at Frank; I intercepted it. Inscribed *NBA,* the ball was marked with the silhouette of a young girl. I didn't tell them about the caves full of sunlight.

Late morning we paddled into the wind toward the research station for supplies, but had to turn back because it was blowing too hard. The sea off the point boiled and tilted.

We tried the wind again in the afternoon. It was a long and open crossing, but with the wind now at our backs we skimmed the waves.

All things happen at once, at the same time. The villagers find a wounded eagle and feed it mice. People change course and an earthquake rewrites the valley. One master follows another. There's raping, killing. Thoughts contain the world. The world contains three men in kayaks. The eagle sits on a pile of sticks in its cage and stares fiercely at whatever approaches. Storm petrels wait. Children come. Demons come. My thoughts react to my gazing at them and open their beaks. The rough sea responds to the increasing wind.

We doubled our strokes when the waves lost order. Red boat to starboard, close to the rocks, the basketball bouncing in a net bag on the deck. The seas rough and disorganised. Wind gusting on our port quarter, then dead astern. The sea churned, confused, white and terrifying, and our small boats rose on tall waves and crashed into valleys, and shuddering towers of spray erupted from surf shattering on the jagged coast.

Concentrate on rudder and wave and paddle stroke, double the strokes.

An arm-length ahead of me, Frank's back was straight, his blind paddle slapping the glassy black roiling surface, almost useless. The eagle in the cage ruffling its feathers. Afraid, yes. Villagers and monks chanting at the dragon festival. A field of dangerous white horses.

A cry, then a shout to starboard. Zhou was trying to turn into the wind, his deck awash, the kayak tipping. Then he fell into the monstrous sea, capsized, clutching the red hull of his boat.

GREAT TOWER GATE

Big seas flipped the red kayak close to the rocks, the basketball was lost and next day, defeated by the storm, we began our drive back to the monastery. I could not speak of what I'd seen. We came upon a car crashed into a ramp railing, police pulling a body from the driver's seat. I'd seen the cave paintings, seen what they were.

Not a bad actor. But I never felt appreciated. You cheered, along with a few others. Actors applauded. Certain directors always called. Not many. Critics remained largely silent. My mother's son, of course. There was that. And not enough fame, recognition, money. There was that. In the end, I couldn't face another audition or screen test: my agent threw up her hands, literally. Her hands in the air, big white flowers. By the time they came down, I had bowed and made my exit, stage left. No. A lengthy period on anti-depressants and a short stint on a psychiatric ward. Bouts of violent behaviour, and the smell of shit, the taste of it, often at night. A sense I'd chosen the wrong role. Not a bad actor, but I gave myself away.

We'd talked and drunk whisky, gone to bed late and slept in. Stepped out of our tent into salt wind. We had paddled our little boats along sea paths, forgetful of everything. How far I'd felt from myself, as if I'd become another kind of being.

Turtledove Tail

I was not helpful to Zhou Yiyuan in the water. The guilt of that. A monk, this monk, must assess the context, the season, and the time of day. Accustomed to quick action, Zhou rescued himself. He swam into a tiny inlet behind a few rocky fangs, and crawled ashore and undressed and wrung out his clothes. I was able eventually to manoeuvre our boat alongside his and tow it into a barnacle-filled crevice and pump the water out of the cockpit, sponging up the last drops. Frank lost his paddle. He sat, eyes closed, in the wind.

Two days later, around midnight, we parked on the river road, just as the bell sounded. Frank hobbled ahead, across the bridge, tapping with his stick.

Central Courtyard

Now back in the valley, back in the lovely valley, I see right away that its magic is all in pieces. I know something.

I was on a train journey zooming east over the roofs of houses, their cluttered yards. Clothesline of billowing plastic bags. Ugly uncut grass. Two children skipping rope. All rolling in black and white. Sky black with wind. White sun on the west horizon. Passengers dozing. Each station brought me closer. Skip. Skip. Skip. Closer.

Chest Centre

Piles of stones and lumber to finish the new storehouse. Can't recognize the faces of monks I've worked beside for years. *Sotto voce*: Now it would be okay to name everything and everyone. Just playing with the idea. But the next word comes, surprise, struggle, swift pain, gravity and light *ta da, you're a monk but you vamoose like a psych patient, like, long term, why not the ten thousand names?*

Our son skipped downstairs to the hall and opened the door and was in the street. The boy weighing his options. Nothing expected. All responsibility waived. Tall flowering trees on the long block. In Amsterdam it rained for a week in June 1989. Our son walked past the trees. The figure smaller and smaller. Shoulders squared for engagement. That was the day I fell out of love. Hours later, tucked in bed, away from the moment, in the middle of the night, sure that evil had taken over the universe, I heard church bells and started to cry, and couldn't easily stop.

JADE HALL

I didn't say anything about the caves, but Frank knew I'd found them. There had been no human forms, only demons: raping, killing, hunting. And now beneath the foundations of the storehouse the workers have found human bones.

PURPLE PALACE

The things around us matter; I love their shapes, even though nine-thousand-nine-hundred-and-ninety-seven are hollow. I love my brush. My broom. My dreams of women. The logjam in the subsiding river. My time in the storehouse library.

"My legs and shoulders ache," I said to Frank. "My kidneys hurt. This morning I could hardly get out of bed."

A snake was sunning itself in the middle of the path, coiled, unaware, and the master stopped in his tracks and turned to me. "I wonder how that is to be written," he said.

"What?"

"That." He lowered his head.

I touched the knuckles of his hand resting on his stick. "You can't see it."

He laughed and stepped over the snake. "Didn't you get out of bed this morning?"

Worry is the opposite of dream. What starts in family, ends in devotion. Instinct rescues itself. Culture looks after the container. If order wrongs chaos, does chaos right order? Where are we? Asylum. Hospital. Sanatorium. Temple. Monastery. Things matter, shape matters. The dying eagle spreads her broken wing. Give the valley a river and a new summer. Give rice a chance to grow. Let the mowed lawn go pointillist with daisies. Let the river shrink to fit its banks. Let humans decrease without suffering. Let fields drain. Let hammers fall. Let the demons through. I didn't lose my son. My wife didn't steal him. Our son grew up.

In the middle of making his latest map, Frank said, in his quiet voice: "It is time to check something."

MAGNIFICENT CANOPY

The ones to be feared are not the bone gatherers in their masks, but those armed with machetes who stand shoulder to shoulder hacking down nettles and canary grass and young bamboo as they slowly advance, eventually to an overgrown path through tall bamboo.

At the end of a day's sweat and labour in the wild land, we came to a black shrine leaning against a basalt wall. We heard splashing overhead, from a waterfall. We let down our tools and sat in the brief clearing we'd made, all gasping from the effort of scything. My legs stung from thorns and knife grass. The shrine roof was green moss a foot deep. Birds were almost deafening in the opened forest. From the beams steam rose, ascending the rock face.

The shrine was empty.

When told, Frank got to his feet and went to see for himself.

My purpose seems to matter less and less each day. Yet it has a shape. A boat, yet not a boat. A bird, yet not a bird. A dragon, yet not. A man, yet not a man. A demon, yet not. One morning soon Imogen will be here.

Jade Pivot

The bellringer's apprentice invited the bell, ran down to help Frank into the tractor, drove from the construction zone to the start of the reclaimed path.

Frank leaned on my shoulder. "Something fishy going on."

We followed the new path to the dark shrine and went inside and sat on the worn boards. "Do you know what?" he said.

"What?"

"I have no idea. Something important."

I did not want to tell him anything yet. "This shrine. Does it have a name?"

He shrugged. "Let's go swimming."

He got to his feet and clutched my fingers and towed me along the shattered path, and then we dropped down to the slow green river and took off our robes and slipped cautiously into the freezing water. I held his hand and we let the current carry us to the deep place where we rolled onto our backs.

The sky fit around branches teeming with birds. We put our feet down and struggled, hand in hand, against the flow, feet slipping on weedy river stones, until we were back at the bank where we'd left our clothes.

"Were your mother and father good to you?" he asked.

"Not really."

"Were they certain about the future?"

"Oh yes. My mother once apologised for living long enough to spend all the money, but she told me not to worry."

"We are like father and son."

"Yes."

"I'm sorry for leaving the world the way it is."

Shape and purpose. Two things that rise simultaneously. Head bowed, in front of the steadily flowing river. The faintest dawn light. Logjam gone. On my way to the temple to see the workmen's progress, stopped by owls calling back and forth among the dark firs — a tall yellow-eyed owl quite close on one branch, another on a higher branch. Two things.

Vancouver.

Once on a beach at dusk, in my twenties and drinking with a party of young teens who had built a fire and were getting loud on beer, I singled out a girl, slim and pretty. Her hair just washed. Her friends reeling.

Family reunion in Amsterdam.

A night long with rain, and the house I'd been given for the duration of the shoot was cold and damp. My ex-wife arrived with the flu. Our son appeared a few days later on his way to an oilrig off the Scottish coast, almost unconscious with jetlag. He had little to say to his mother, and wouldn't speak to me. The tension in the house was unbearable.

He woke early that morning, came bounding downstairs, and accused us both of selfishness, of faking this *family time*, of never caring about him, never allowing him to make up his own mind. As if we were united, at that time, in anything. As if the family was still intact. In that seventeenth-century house on *Zielstraat* he accused us of utter failure, professional and social, and particularly in our relationship. Unsuccessful, unsuccessful. "And terrible, like totally, in the domestic sphere."

I asked him how he was going to fare on an oilrig with his teen-speak and large vocabulary, his tall bony frame and soft white skin. "You are nineteen. You are too cocky. You won't last five minutes. Your childish accusations of us are really for yourself. It will do you good to fail."

"Fuck you," he said.

I said it was time, in that case, for him to get out of our lives.

My ex turned and walked down the tall narrow hallway to her room.

Our son slouched off along the street and I stood trembling at the open door until he vanished in fog and traffic.

I'm pretty sure we knew right away it was a final failure (without consulting at the time or afterwards). My ex caught the first flight out, back to her own life; I was woken by church bells, and over the next days, between shoots, talked long distance with oilrig officials, trying to get hold of my son. But I did not reach him and have not spoken to him or seen him since.

A law, code, taboo, has been broken. I'm afraid of getting caught. I danced with the girl on the beach. The undertow of this memory has warped every desire, turned it into a heavy, loaded, ripe, loose, tumultuous thing. Our dance ended with a short illicit self-complete — what? The memory disintegrates into a ravening core, infinitely dense and increasingly radio-active, a singing darkness I must never unfold. A yearning so colossal that if dwelt on would dismantle my grasp on purpose and shape.

Fingerprints in ash-dust on the thighs of white bellbottoms.

I cried a long time for Song Wei.

Romance is the waiting-word, or some relic root of *romance*, some shadow, some obsolete ritualistic pre-lingual shade just outside memory.

Grunt it. Locate it. *Romance. Fuck you.* Every word is a marker, a crossroad. Open your eyes. *Demon.* Familiar, this rising from the depths. Look! Look! The river. Daylight. Two owls. The beach. Amsterdam.

Whatever you name the other, do it quickly, before the other names you. Quickdraw McGraw. Axiomatic DNA. *Soul Street.*

When I started this record, *Zielstraat* was a wide summer avenue, the lawns accidental, well-watered and green with promise, even the doctors optimistic and in love. Now disappointments have hurt my heart. We know where spring love has gone. Hades stole her down a crack in the earth and keeps her in his cave, one eye to the spy-hole.

So of course the newfound shrine, old indeed, its purpose lost, will be re-abandoned, and the recovered path allowed to go wild. We can't afford to believe we own everything. No, we can't.

RIDGE SPRING

This morning at prayer there were ten quail chicks by the forest path behind the temple, by noon two, now only one. After silent contemplation of the chick and the parent birds I no longer want or need my mother, father, wife, son. May not need or want desire. I don't know who creates this life, with all its notional success and failure, or how ten became one so quickly, how one has survived so completely. But I knew one unnameable and unique scurrying dot.

I don't know what things are, not any longer. Although gaps between things are frequent — nothing to joke about — and words don't matter, and brush strokes are superfluous, I can't help continuing. The past is close-formed, like a maze parallel to what we think of as reality. Do we really want to know what we've burrowed ourselves out of? A long and largely unobserved life, a stay in the country?

Villeggiatura.

What is it in night's silence that we're still anxious to back away from? Even settle for nursing home, full-meal cafeteria, on-call support, arboretum, well-forested grounds. The true object of wandering is unimaginable escape. *Surely*, says a voice, *what we are trying to distract ourselves from can't be all that bad.*

Sauce Spoon

A retired actor friend (successful!), after his wife died, fitted out a cliff cave in Oregon — hidden entrance, step-down porch, triple-glazed windows, ocean views — and sealed himself in: no more public soliloquy. "Look," he said of the cave's systems. "A flick of a switch and this sucker is independent of everything."

"Power reduced to narcissism," I said.

And me? I only want to ply my old trade one last time. Fuck the shoals of consciousness, *n'est-ce pas*? The woman, Imogen, aka Aphrodite, Persephone, Eurydice, aka *the girl*, may only exist in movies. Or caves. Though if she's part of my purpose, she will hold my shape, and something in me thinks it is tall with blood. What venal purpose, indeed, hides behind the act of writing? Acting was my game.

And if the animals come to hear me, no adjectives or co-stars will be celebrated. Adverbs and special effects will be nullified. Gently, I will sing to myself.

And so I asked Frank about the nature of evil, expecting some reply, some kind of simple answer.

He stopped rocking.

We were sitting in the dirt, in the foundations of the new storehouse after work had ceased for the day, and we seemed to be waiting.

There we were, all romance: monks in the empty temple, masters in their cave, Zhou Yiyuan in his new truck — all our prayers, tools, cables, windows, and scaffolding half-alive.

JULY

Long Strong   Governing

AT MIDNIGHT, FRANK COMES TO LEAD ME PAST my sleeping brother monks to the garden door. "Go in, but say nothing."

And so into the garden, a perfect replica, water and shadows built around a single point.

When I was ten and displaced six thousand miles, the path home from school led under power lines through brambles, where a woman's murdered body had once been hidden. I remember cranking foolscap onto the spindle of the manual typewriter, the urge to get things down before they vanished. The words undulated under the clock-radio's telescoping lamp. Then the silver screen, school plays — the mitochondria of signification — and the past is full, complete, dark, and cannot be opened.

In *Songs of Innocence*, Blake spent pages on his lost-and-found girl, but for the lost boy: "The night was dark, no father was there; / The child was wet with dew."

The smooth track curled round the garden lake past invisible forms. Let me list what's important. My son, my lost unknowable accent, this job of reducing everything to a single point, dark old desire. I passed the salt tracing of an extinct Egyptian town, a Greek temple, the arena, a vicious sea, the basketball with the silhouette girl. For what play?

Lumbar Shu

I found a pomegranate on the temple steps. Frank was waiting inside.

He raised his head. "Come in, come in. Choose a place to sit. I have another letter."

The bird who loves Quan Yin flew into her right eye and found a perch on Stomach-1, Container of Tears. I opened the envelope.

"She will come in two weeks," I said.

"She will see some changes."

Lumbar Yang Pass

We meet daily in the shade of New East Shrine before descending to the river to swim.

The slow movement. The slow movement. The slow movement. The garden writing sessions use all my other time. The past has hiccups and I'm trying to hold my breath. I recognize nothing in Frank's latest maps. Sometimes, as now, I simply watch his gentle narrow kind face, more familiar than my own.

Life Gate

Last night I woke to the scream and unhooked my drum from the wall and went out into the warm darkness and met Zhou Yiyuan on the bridge and he led me to the nut grove where, in the clearing, we sat on our haunches side by side. He got me to tap my heartbeat on the skin while he sang and the sun rose and opened the valley point by point, deeper and deeper red.

This long day was made of sessions and chopping wood, sweating in the hot sun, and a simple bowl of rice with broth.

Our food stores are replenished; we give the extra aid parcels to departing villagers and river refugees.

We hiked along the river, Frank's stick finding the uneven ground for his limping foot, and undressed under the willow. His pouch belly, smooth yet wrinkled at the edges, his penis a white dowel, his balls pendant eggs in grizzled fur.

We held hands and let the current take us downriver, just to the fast water before the bridge, then waded home close to the bank. I lent him my arm as we stumbled over the slippery stones. Clothes warm on our skin. Another fresh return.

Suspended Pivot

Zhou and the North Valley abbot stood in the shade of the warrior tree. Men stripped to the waist worked stone and wood for the new storehouse. The location of each timber is determined by the old stone base. The human bones have been set aside, waiting to be laid at the back of the cave, and boulders fallen from the mountain have been bulldozed out of the way to stand guard against the bamboo forest.

The earthquake in the garden has mimicked the one outside. Here industry isn't an obstacle to anything but solitude.

"A ceasefire has been signed!" Zhou Yiyuan shouted.

Cheers from the workmen and a few villagers.

"We will have three years of famine."

The abbot shook his head.

Imogen is coming. Between her and me is the short time remaining and what it contains (if time can contain anything) — geographic distance, corrupted history, explosive fuels, flight technology, pollen, dust, pharmaceuticals. Such un-animal-like things. *Romance* will be removed.

Centre of the Spine

We walk around the garden wall. Swim in the river, look out for whirlpools. Zhou Yiyuan has claimed Song Wei's daughter; she is a nomad among nomads.

Central Pivot

I crossed the bridge and walked the highway to the next village and thought of my sister last time I saw her, a strong solitary woman planting tomatoes under the huge cedars of her cottage, her restless past behind her. Dust flew up when trucks rumbled past. Heavy skies, black to the north, presaged rain.

Once upon a time, when the four of us still slept under the same roof and I had just learned to drive and was out cruising at night, I picked up two girl hitchhikers. Spoke with the girl in the passenger seat beside me, a stranger. To find out later it was my sister. Back at the bridge a flash in the reeds caught my eye — jewel, tin, glass — and I tripped and fell to my knees. We'd carried on a conversation in the dark and I had not recognised her.

Only what's important. The bridge. A mother's wishes for her children. Home. I crawled to the edge and looked down at the shining bone and wing of a bird snagged in the weeds, tugged by the current. *A gap called Change between the body and the wing.*

Sinew Contraction

Past the spring shrine to North Gate. Dawn birds chattering and bathing. Returned to the courtyard for meditation, but couldn't stay focussed. The routine and place shifting, dry and warm weather. Frank and Zhou Yiyuan trading places. I know what is adrift.

"My energy is too great for working on others."

Frank passed without answering. Our exchange was antique and only gleamed briefly. A felt thing. A cloud through the forest.

Before sleep, I gather in all the objects I brought with me, all I've collected since, a small hoard. I don't know what to do with it. Friends. Bowls of tea. A dream the master dreamed.

Reaching Yang

Cancer, in the world since the beginning, rampant cells, Dad in the flow, Mum anxious on the bank. Waking up disrupted the dream and I leaned back and scanned the forest from the open shrine. No one.

This afternoon session a leopard wandered the perimeter of our circle, pawed the garden wall, then leapt over. A hawk flew from the new well to the warrior tree. The cat was changing its life. The bird shrieked. Qi pulsed at my fingertips, *fire, wood* — a powerful surge between my fingers and the monk's skin. Our lives quitting the west, quitting the east. The sky a ferocious blue bowl.

SPIRIT TOWER

Zhou Yiyuan assembled the monks behind the temple and invited the bell. The North Valley abbot led a chant.

"There is not enough money to rebuild the storehouse," Zhou Yiyuan said. "There are options, none easy. Businessmen would like to buy the land to build a lodge and retreat centre. These men are constructing a series of factories in North Valley."

The North Valley abbot looked round at the rest of us, embarrassed, pale. Thinner than when I saw him last fall.

"They want you to move to the mountain," Zhou continued. "They want to open the monastery to visitors. A few monks would remain. The shrines would be protected. The garden would be opened." His fingers held the edges of his too-long sleeves. "They will finish the storehouse. They have promised that." He looked at the abbot.

"We must meditate on the possibilities," said the abbot.

SPIRIT PATH

No sleep because of the heat, and the problems multiplying, and no rain yet. We wade into the river, soaking our robes several times a day. Meditate all afternoon. In the evening, I watch herons walking slowly across the garden's shallow lake, back and forth, the light falling sideways, red from the western sky.

My gut worse, the pain intense — life a list and gloss and letting go. Yet such clarity near the sealed garden in the open garden. A shift in my spirit. You are still with me, thanks for that. Not long now.

Then fitful sleep, nonviable dust sifting to the bottom of things, nothing to fathom.

Body Pillar

She is coming. The crews have mysteriously vanished, replaced by birds in large white flocks, and tonight five fires are burning — the last of the villagers' dwellings by the river — at this time of year a dangerous event. Acrid smoke everywhere. The fires refused to spread, despite the dryness and the heat, and they burned themselves out by morning.

I took a path through the paddies to the abandoned storehouse to watch Zhou Yiyuan's Warrior Tree Ceremony. Two women elders from the departing village linked hands; between them Zhou turned a complete circle, a dwarf between ordinary women, a child playing Blind Man's Buff.

Tock-tock of woodpeckers in the nut trees across the river. I was waiting for the year of waiting to catch a spark. *He feels heavy though his heart is old bleached wood exposed to the summer sun.* Nothing left to accomplish, but Imogen will come next week. Something still for you to witness.

Way of Happiness (Kiln Path)

A circle. A square. A circle. A desk lost in brambles, priceless measuring instruments in the top drawer. Callipers, scale, meter, level. A book with uncut pages; I open the board: the frontispiece is a woodcut called *Childhood.*

Silken movements, tracking the body's twelve-part river, meridian by meridian, then holding Kiln Path, the hole below the first thoracic vertebra. This is the route back: retracing paths through winter to find the snow-covered entrance to the cave, crawling hind-first into an ice tunnel, through fall and out the other side to summer. Winter before winter, fall before fall.

Please don't let this be a false start to the mountain. What is mine? My ancestors' birth dates, every day of the year? Anything else?

Here's a beautiful drinking glass and a few inches of golden liquid Dad blamed me for stealing. Blamed me for stealing the whisky and borrowing the car and returning it dirty. Half-jokes. The house was dark. It was just before dusk and I'd been out playing all day. The air gentle through the sheer curtains: summer rain on tarmac.

"Don't forget to be good," Dad said. He was resting in his favourite chair.

I was about to step into my own life. I needed to think, needed to work through a last few shapes, but there he was.

Great Hammer

The river was once called Red. Red River, from the cinnabar leaching from the hill mines. Higher, it had a different name, the accounts vary — Snake, Rushing, Green — and toward the sea it was called Black because no light penetrated the high walls of the gorge. Old maps. But no one refers to it by name anymore. It is golden now, from the pollen that floats on its surface.

I'm avoiding something. Some part of my life looming and not wanting to be named. When I close my eyes I see a perfect red half-open rose.

Mute Gate

Rose in a narrow square glass vase. I was reading a script at the table and you were behind me. Then I was on stage, sweeping the kitchen floor, clumsy with my arm in a sling, and you were in front of me. (I broke it, remember, leaping from my front door.) My son once tried to piggyback my wife late one night just before bed. *Step on a crack.* My father showed me the high rose window setting the air on fire.

I am waiting.

Expecting cogs to engage through a shift in the orientation of my soul to simple gravity. What do I really possess? My poor teeth. Two whole arms. Feet on the ground. What is it about Imogen that draws me and promises transformation? She is a public figure (I was a public figure), a screen figure (I was a screen figure); she seeks depth of experience (I seek depth). *We are English.*

I remember a film, years ago, sitting bolt upright in the communal dark, alive with lust and longing, staring at the screen, the air on fire. She was texture and light only, texture and light. Vancouver afterwards, grey buildings and wet sidewalks, seemed flimsy and tawdry, too complex and detailed. *One rainy summer afternoon.*

Then recognising her in the little boat, led ashore by monks, green water streaming at her feet, summer clouds blowing north, *one rainy summer afternoon*, the whiteness of her skin and hair and dress, the sun haloing her — I could not push out a single word, not even hello.

WIND MANSION

Closer! In the air, crossing water. Quick, what's left to jettison? What do I possess? Could possessions be reduced to longing and uncertainty? As a child I waited for food, for Mum and the pussy-cat, *night-night, sleep tight* (the record still occupies a drawstring purse in the valise). I waited for my dad. I waited for adoration, acclamation. I waited for money and acceptance until I understood what they were good for. She is in the air now, crossing an ocean, flying toward the valley. Time and space wrestle like a couple of greased kids, one shy, one robust. I am waiting for grace and a flint. For *picaresque* to meet *romance*. Her foot on the bridge.

I swam with Frank, old dear fool, and we drifted as usual, then he said this may be our last swim. Fractures in the bridge pilings, in the footings, visible now the river level was low. As we dried ourselves, he clapped for my attention, as if I was blind, then smiled and said: "Are you paying your best mind?" After dressing, we walked to the bridge, but did not cross. We stood in hot sun, listening to the water, to the voices of children.

I was not able to sleep more than a few hours last night. Eating was out of the question. I went through the day's routine in a state of extended awareness, even to the knowledge that many parts were engaged elsewhere. What to do with these fragments of a long life, inside the valley, outside the valley, these mazy squiggles? Delete the non-essential bits? How can we tell what doesn't matter?

Zhou Yiyuan touched my sleeve. "You remember when we met here?"

I scuffed my feet against the rough fibres of the new bridge deck. I watched him raise his long arms into the air, heavy with pride. We stared into the murky water streaming past the pylons. The cracks in cement, stones working loose. Upstream, children were swimming in the pool where an hour earlier Frank and I also had felt the silk-cool water on our skin.

When I fell, doubled over in pain, others gathered around me, the monks and villagers.

"I'm okay. Fine. I'm fine."

Imogen is the single point, high above the earth; hers is a short path amid billions of stars. She is like you, her path like yours.

Today, like all days, was built on ritual, prayer and chanting and long hands on bodies. Invisible parts were in flux, of course, waiting for a spark, waiting for flight. How much we regret losing our bodies' beauty and youth and strength.

Frank stood below us on the dock, his grey narrow face lopsided, lips curving, pointing.

Brain's Door

The boy's father again, down by the first bridge piling, as always distracted, smoking and looking off upstream, downstream, while no small boy plays quietly at his side. Whatever comes at him (monks, soldiers, double agents) will be spotted long before it arrives, because he did not know how to protect his son.

Smoke from the offering fire, rippling shadow-lines of sun through trees in front of the cave, reminds me of the lighting design for a play I once was in: drunk farmers laughing and nudging one another and sharing cigarettes on one side of the stage, while on the other a projector threw light at a threadbare sheet hung between potted trees.

I worked on two monks and discovered in each a shame, a sense of not deserving. One thought he was detestably ugly; the other believed he was too old to feel the passion he felt for a young monk.

The monastery, its future uncertain, seems unmoored. The unbearable heat of the past two weeks has burst into rain and slow rivers of mud. Long tendrils of willow drag in the water. The valley wobbles and may vanish in the night. High on the mountain is a grey smoke smudge. Crews with shovels trench around the storehouse, pushing soft wet earth. Papers have been signed. Frank's smile could mean anything. Zhou Yiyuan and the abbot entertain businessmen who come in private cars and stay a few hours, visiting the warrior tree and one shrine, before recrossing the bridge, their shoes caked with mud. Experts in lab coats are resorting and tagging the bones. An architect from the city is angry with the ditch crew. Shouts echo from on top of our hill. The bell keeps perfect time. The bus flashes by, windows crammed with faces. I count seventeen sky gods outraged by the forces working the margins.

Unyielding Space

She is here. Sleeping. Young skinny crows scream and scream.

Behind the Crown

Zhou Yiyuan and the abbot guide her around the damage and the rebuilding to the cave fire.

In meditation I look for accidents to hurl us together.

"The grass is heavy with seed," Frank told me. "Go and sit inside her room."

Hundred Meetings

A boy ran down the mountain path shouting, then he vanished in trees. Reappeared on top of our small hill, slight body charging the spring shrine. From the shadows of the temple, he emerged, wings flapping for arms. Storehouse workmen shaded their eyes to watch him fall to his knees by the well.

He had a golden eagle.

The valley quiet in the sun and steam.

Down by the river, new migrants were bent over, ankle-deep in slime. Picking small objects from alluvium, they filled their bags.

The door grated against stone and I stood watching her face, pale and slow against the brown pillow, streaming with bright summer light.

"What is happening?" Her lashes raised, incandescent blue eyes on me, shadows tilting.

"It is a boy." I stepped into the green sunny hut.

She smiled like a child. "You are still here."

We listened to voices laughing in high summer. "A boy has come down the mountain with an eagle. A golden eagle."

In Front of the Crown

I sat at her side and watched her sleep. She is beautiful. We kneeled together and she allowed me to look into those blue eyes. I don't know what mine were doing but there was mild apology in hers, and pleasure. The boy. The eagle. "I have been thinking," she said. "I have been thinking about you all night."

Fontanel Meeting

I couldn't contain myself as we swam in the river, Frank and I. We drifted and I watched Imogen pause on the bridge. This was the culmination. Trees and river were green phenomena, ceiling blue-and-white *trompe l'oeul*. A steady breeze supported squadrons of iridescent turquoise dragonflies; shadows flickered on bleached river grasses; seedheads burst against the sky.

She stood still, fingers on the rail, on a high platform; new lines round her small mouth.

Our play beginning.

Water gently dripped into the glossy river from Frank's sunburned hands as he held them out for balance.

"She's on the bridge, Frank, looking along the river, and she can't see us."

His whole face opened, a kingfisher's quick passage. "Now what will you do?"

Accumulations of human seasons dispersed into summer dark.

Upper Star

The boy sat on a long white stone near the old well, holding a feather. I saw him and crossed from the warrior tree through the ripening plums, to his side. White ash whirled like snow. Ruined books and prints were burning, the texts of our work. Salvaged documents were to be moved by stages to a city vault.

One moment the boy was wrestling the eagle, the next he saw his dad fall. They'd been climbing the mountain for two days, crossing to a safe place. His dad had heard there was work north; cities were being built.

"The eagle attacked him." The boy mimed wingspread, talons.

All set to go home, the little pain in my side hot, wind rustling the flags, the birds singing, the bell and machines chatting. As soon as I raised my arm, the grieving spy joined us.

No need to go on. There is no reason to stop. A new moon and the monastery at night is still, with Imogen asleep in its grounds. If she's the river, I'm the valley, and she's the boy on the mountain. If I'm a patient, we are actors, and nothing if not adaptive. Skirt the crumbling cliff, go further into chaos; for now the ground feels solid. Our lives overlap.

And then through vast darkness I staggered up the mountain and stared down at the valley where she slept, a snug earthworm, heart of centuries. My son would arrive with his own son and see the new storehouse, the monastery, incomplete, and tell me what was whole, what was a fragment. We were his fragments! Monastery, mountain and river. From the ridge, through the trees I could see a light dancing at the edge of the west plum border.

The nut grove above the river was where we met, in the flattened grass where deer had slept, mist a tongue over water, the sun just risen. She greeted Zhou Yiyuan, who kept glancing up at her face as he showed her the battle sites, and then faded away. Inkling of "nut grove." Inkling of "the two of us." And a jasmine vine.

She was restless, then calm, then up to pluck a bud. "My last film was a failure. Never accept roles like that!"

She fell on her back, her forehead troubled. Sun climbed into the clearing.

My finger, heavy, hovered over *Sanjiao-3*, wood-fire, *shu*-stream. Her belly opened. The heart's minister, *Zhongzhu*, abandoned Central Islet; scarlet robes flickered through the trees.

The doctors cross their lawn. So I'm free to go.

I followed her along the smooth track through a tangle of vines back to the river.

Next morning *she* led *me* past shrines and battle sites to the green nut grove, our brief settlement, cathedral of buzzing bees, to Mum and Dad, my sister and her child. My son's cry never woke me; my wife always heard him; she always heard his cry. But now I hear him, if only a word, and the river, the cave, the grass, sun, reed bed, the bamboo spirit, Imogen, everything slips away. Clouds race the day-moon.

Spirit Courtyard

Song Wei and Frank fly away, low over River Temple and Mound Bell, through the North Gate

White Crevice

and up to North Pass and nameless darkness. "Not so strange," she whispered.

Hall of Impression

Fresh paths filling with leaves again, too quickly for a monk to sweep. My old broom's settled high between two tangled stems of the jasmine vine. Why not cast all this as high as I can one last time before I leave? Stop work and listen to the bell ringing the end of the summer day?

Made in England spells and spells cast in Canada and spells in China. Nests I tried to make. Knots I tried to unravel. Points I tried to find. Stop work and listen to the bell.

It's the rose window! How can mind know bell from glass, what shines from what sings? I must remember it isn't the rose we made, it's the rose window. I must remember to replace the plank across the ditch going home.

— Vancouver 03/21/2012